PEACE BREAKS OUT
JOHN KNOWLES

"What a magnificent writer he is! . . . There's an air of mystery in this lean, well-formed book. Every line counts, and reader can trust author without fear of disappointment."

—*Newsday*

"Spare prose . . . and skillful plotting which blends the routine and the remarkable."

—*The New York Times Book Review*

"Knowles effectively uses the microcosm of a boarding school to highlight the manipulative dark side of the human heart, which is never fully eradicated by the sacrificial violence of war."

—*Library Journal*

"Pleasing, disturbing, and very good indeed . . . not only a worthy successor to *A Separate Peace*, it can stand alone."

—*Baltimore Sun*

Bantam Books by John Knowles

PEACE BREAKS OUT

A SEPARATE PEACE

PEACE BREAKS OUT

JOHN KNOWLES

BANTAM BOOKS
TORONTO · NEW YORK · LONDON · SYDNEY · AUCKLAND

This low-priced Bantam Book
has been completely reset in a type face
designed for easy reading, and was printed
from new plates. It contains the complete
text of the original hard-cover edition.
NOT ONE WORD HAS BEEN OMITTED.

PEACE BREAKS OUT

A Bantam Book / published by arrangement with
Holt, Rinehart and Winston

PRINTING HISTORY

Holt, Rinehart & Winston edition published March 1981
Bantam edition / October 1982

ISBN 0-553-22580-4

Published simultaneously in the United States and Canada

PRINTED IN THE UNITED STATES OF AMERICA

O   0 9 8 7 6 5 4 3

In Memoriam:

THORNTON WILDER

Novelist, Playwright, Inspiring Teacher

MOTHER COURAGE: Bells! What are the bells for, middle of the week!

CHAPLAIN: What are they shouting?

YOUNG MAN: It's peace.

CHAPLAIN: Peace!

MOTHER COURAGE: Don't tell me peace has broken out—when I've just gone and bought all these supplies!

—*Bertolt Brecht*

PEACE
BREAKS
OUT

1

The Devon School had endured in the mind of Pete Hallam throughout his combat years in Italy as a close-held memory of peacetime. Its balanced eighteenth-century houses, its red-brick no-nonsense nineteenth-century dormitories, its elaborate neo-Georgian twentieth-century class buildings stood in his infantryman's recollection as untainted and unthreatened and reassuring, a valued part of his past back in New Hampshire. He could never lapse so far into sentimentality as to think he was "fighting for Devon" or for anything else as a matter of fact except self-survival and an end to fighting, but the image of the halcyon lanes and broad-sweeping Playing Fields was a steady focus for his memories of peacetime as he had known it, his particular microcosm, serene and unchanged.

And now, in September 1945, here he was literally returning to Devon as an instructor in American History and a member of the Physical Education staff.

At the town of Hampton he turned off Route 1 and headed the few miles inland from the Atlantic coast to the village of Devon. He drove his 1940 Ford station wagon with a particular sense of contentment through the rolling, wooded country. It still faintly surprised him to see a countryside totally untouched by the defacements of war. His eyes had grown so used to buildings reduced to shambles, roads like quagmires, fields blasted into hellholes, that these vistas of rich meadows, neat farmhouses and orderly woods looked fake to him, stage scenery.

So the dreary, ferocious years he had spent in the Infantry, the shrapnel holes in his left leg, the searing months as a prisoner of war, could at least be thought to have some redeeming meaning: this whole continent had escaped unscathed from a world at war. Only North American people had been damaged, killed; all the buildings and all the fields remained untouched. That, he had to admit, was something to show for what he and everyone else overseas had had to go through.

And, after all, he had survived it far better than many others: he was not crazy as two men in his company had become; he had not gone deaf; his hands still shook but not very much; he no longer had so many nightmares.

Pete drove down a slope and into the little village, crossing the small bridge which spanned the Devon River just before it fell over a small waterfall and mingled with the tidewater Naguamsett River. He circled the lacy, cast-iron bandstand in the center of town and turned left, very soon passing into the precincts of the school.

Of course it looked smaller than he had visualized it. Everything looked smaller. Perhaps life itself was going to be smaller now, now that the great and terrible drama was over, all of the dead were buried, and the victors of the Second World War were commencing to see one another as enemies, the earlier enemies having been vanquished.

The school was just as beautiful as he remembered it. The great trees, the dignified commons and courtyards, the gray-white Gothic Chapel, a miniature cathedral with its imposing bell tower which reached a little higher than the competing cupolas of the First Academy Building and the Administration Building, all so exactly like themselves that once again he thought involuntarily: A stage set: men will strike it and cart it off in a minute.

But the school had been here for a century and a half and seemed likely to endure at least another century or so. It was not a snobbish school; it did not rely on the rich for its continuity, although several philanthropists had heavily endowed it. Devon was larger—seven hundred students—and much older and more deeply rooted than the St. Grottlesex schools, those Episcopalian imitations of Eton and Harrow. Devon was sort of Congregationalist when it came to religion, which it did not often do, with a predominantly Protestant student body mixed with numerous Catholics and a sprinkling of Jews.

Pete pulled up in front of Pembroke House, a four-square white colonial manse fronting a large ell where the students lived. Mr. Roscoe Bannerman Latch of the Latin Department lived here in the principal faculty quarters with his wife, and there was a small annex apartment on the ground floor which would now become the sole and perhaps permanent domicile of Mr. Peter Hallam, Devon '37, soldier home from the wars.

The first thing he noticed, entering his apartment, was a fair-sized fireplace in the far wall, and he felt a small, atavistic ripple of pleasure at the sight of it, the hearth: barracks and bivouacs didn't have them. There were three scatter rugs on the floor, a rather battered desk and chair, a worn and comfortable-looking easy chair by the fireplace, bookshelves, lamps, a couple of tables, two framed prints of Harvard scenes, narrow sash windows, a low ceiling, and a general sense of old-fashioned functionality. Off the living room–office were a small kitchen and a bedroom which, while modest, outstripped anything the Army had provided.

He carried in his bags and boxes and put them in the middle of the floor. Opening the first box, which had been stored at his parents' home in Western Massachusetts all these years, he found staring up at him a photograph of the Dartmouth hockey team, 1940. Pete lifted it out; he looked then very much as he looked now, high cheekbones and firm features; with his brown-black hair and light blue eyes and normal expression of decisiveness he supposed he looked like the typical Ivy League hockey player. He still looked today very much like that twenty-one-year-old college boy in the team photograph; the only significant change was a masked fatigue behind the firm-featured face now; he still looked just like a bright hockey player, who had, however, been what the French called *excédé*, pushed beyond all normal limits of exertion and stress. On the surface he seemed just as athletic and energetic as ever; behind that appearance were concealed the damaged leg and the psyche of which too much had been asked.

Standing next to him in the photograph, looking slightly maniacal, was Mel Hendrickson, the best, fastest skater on the team, also the practical joker and general cutup, the one who saw the comedy in everything. He was killed by a land mine soon after the American Army crossed the Rhine River. By that time in the European campaign it was obvious that the war in Europe was won. But it was not yet over, and that discrepancy destroyed Mel Hendrickson.

Behind them in the picture stood Brooks Brewster, second-string goalie, looking squat and rather mean. His nickname was The Mole. He left his meanness on the ice and was just another jokester: perhaps they had all been. Pete's eyes swept the ranks of the hockey team and almost all of them in his memory seemed to be chuckling or whooping or grinning. At least that was how he remembered them. Mole Brewster's B-17 went down in flames over the Ruhr.

In the front row was Joe Raynor, at the time absolutely bent on becoming a reporter, journalist, foreign correspondent, columnist, newspaper pundit. He died in a hospital in New Guinea of some virulent infection.

Pete put the photograph on the shelf and reached for another in the box. It was of an extremely pretty blonde young woman gazing rather purposefully out at him from a silver frame: his ex-wife, Joan. He hated to look at that face; he had once loved it, her. It was unsettling to look at her now. Why was she so pretty? How could nature allow her to be so pretty, promising, idealistic-looking? The picture had been taken four years earlier and no doubt she was still just as pretty, she of the slightly husky, captivating voice, of the superb legs, of the treachery. He plunged the photograph back in the box.

The last picture he lifted out was a triptych, three linked frames of family pictures. On the left were his mother and father at their twentieth wedding anniversary party, he looking more like a diplomat than a successful businessman in his dinner jacket, his mother in a long lace dress looking just like the Lady with a capital *L* that she always had been. The center picture was the Birches, their home in Lenox, brick, neo-colonial, spacious, with many wooded acres around it, an ideal place for four sons to grow up.

His three brothers were in the final photo: Mike, three years older than Pete, Yale, Naval commander, now about to enter law practice in Providence; George, one year Pete's senior—4-F because of poor eyesight, otherwise the "Perfect Specimen" as his football buddies had dubbed him—now a doctor in Bangor, Maine; and finally Teddy, two years younger than Pete, supposed to be the most gifted of them, played the piano very well, liked to paint, swimming star, lover boy according to his classmates.

He was dead. Teddy had been killed liberating Cannes, picked off by a sniper as he and his squad were advancing cautiously along the Croisette from the Palm Beach Casino toward the Carlton Hotel. He had been a very good boy, Teddy, reflected Pete, a very promising, ardent, talented kid. And now Cannes was free.

There was a knock at the door. Before he could reach it the door swung ajar and Mr. Latch's slightly mad head thrust in—hooked nose, overstimulated watery blue eyes, uncontrolled white-red hair, flushed, excited expression. "My boy, my boy, am I interrupting anything? Come over to our digs, will you? Glass of sherry. Debo's worried you're lonesome already. Are you? Of course not. Sentimental woman, too many novels. Flaubert, *Anna Karenina*, Henry *James*. Ugh. Come on over, want to? Not finished unpacking? Do that later."

There was no stopping Roscoe Latch once set on a course, whether it was dragging Pete away for a glass of sherry or undermining the previous Headmaster's authority. He had been Pete's Latin teacher during his Upper Middle year at Devon. From him Pete had learned what the words "discipline" and "precision" and "ceaseless energy" and "personal authority" really meant.

Roscoe Latch ushered him across the little entrance hall and Mrs. Latch welcomed him with a bright, intellectual smile. Her brown-gray hair was parted in the middle and pulled back into a bun. This set off her patrician, prowlike features and her aware green-gray eyes.

"Mrs. Latch—" he began.

"Do call me Deborah, now we're house-sharing. *Don't* call me 'Debo.' Only Roscoe inflicts that on me. It sounds like an Italian water closet or something."

Their living room had the low ceiling of the eighteenth century. Undoubtedly this large room had once been two or three small ones. One of the original fireplaces survived, as did the wide-plank flooring. The furniture consisted of bits and pieces, old, new, mostly small, well kept but worn, like, as a matter of fact, the two Latches. September sunshine shone through sash windows looking toward the Chapel.

Pete accepted a glass of sherry and took a small wooden chair, Roscoe sat in another and Deborah established herself on a couch next to the fireplace.

"Here you are back from the wars!" Roscoe exclaimed cheerily in his swallowed, marbles-in-the-mouth British voice. "And I'm sure you'll find little old Devon a risible backwater after the great world and the great war."

Thank God there are people still left in the world using the word "risible," thought Pete. Maybe if I'm really lucky I'll never have to hear that eternal army four-letter word or any of its variations again. He had not until this moment realized how bone-tired he was of GI talk, its poverty, its repetitions, its glumness.

"It's good to be back," Pete said energetically, "and a little unreal. Is that really the Chapel over there where I sat every morning for four years, or is it cardboard? Are the bells really still in that tower, and do they still ring? It's a little hard to believe somehow."

Deborah was squinting sympathetically across at him. "But doesn't all seem trivial here to you now, beside the point, *precieux*?"

"Not at all," said Pete, grinning. "I'm just so damn glad places like this are left, after so much got blasted away."

"Doubtless," began Roscoe in his trickiest and most urbane tone, "Latin has revealed itself to you in all its unutterable irrelevance."

"Sir," Pete said reflexively and was then struck with the thought that now that he too was a Master at Devon "sir" might be inappropriate, "to read Latin you have to know how to think and to keep complicated rules in your head and to relate some things to other things, and, well, I never have been better trained anywhere for using my mind than in your Latin class."

Roscoe chortled and coughed, flushing. Had Pete embarrassed or touched the impermeable Roscoe Latch?

Recovering, Roscoe looked across at him in his birdlike way. Then he said with his usual cheerfulness, "I fear fewer and fewer people—students, faculty, trustees—will agree with you and me. Latin will go the way of Moral Philosophy and Alchemy and reading entrails. You and I know it is superb conditioning of the mental muscles, we know how simple it makes learning the Romance languages, we are aware of its impact on everyday English. But they, the new men? This is the Century of the Common Man, everyone says so. The Common Man, studying Latin? Not bloody likely. But I," an accepting sigh, "shall be retired in three more years and . . ."

"And," Deborah took up the sentence, "you have had a remarkable and valuable career, and Peter here is one more proof of it."

"I hope I am," said Pete a shade uncomfortably.

Consciously and firmly closing off that subject by shifting in his chair and putting his chin in his hand, Roscoe said, "You're going to find the students rather different from your day, you know."

"Am I?" said Pete. "How?"

"Rather more serious, funnily enough, a bit 'traumatized,' in the cant psychiatric word, by the war they have just missed becoming involved in. The world has been an amazing and stupefying and extremely dangerous place all through their adolescence and it has left its brand on them. They're not as happy-go-lucky as you boys were, Depression or no Depression. They're tougher, somehow." He chortled. "They *are* boys, of course, and boys *will be* boys. Two of them climbed the Chapel steeple last year, on the outside, belaying, I believe it's called." He ran his fingers through his scrappy hair. "But all the same, they have been marked by this war. I believe they feel that anything, anything at all, may possibly happen to them in their lives after all that. The sky's the limit, and so is hell. If I had to put it in one word, the difference between students of your day and of today, the word would be 'aware.' You weren't aware; they are."

"Well I guess I'm aware now!" Pete burst out with a laugh. Too bad I had to walk the length of Italy through the bombs and the rain, get shot up and captured to become aware, he added to himself.

"You were rather good at sports, I seem to remember," Roscoe observed with suave vagueness.

Knows every position I ever played on every team here, Pete suddenly realized with amusement. Full of tricks, sir, aren't you? "Not bad," Pete concurred.

"And ah," put in Deborah, "you'll be doing coaching as well as teaching. The whole man," she added with a kind of abstract admiration. "*Mens sana in corpore sano.*"

"I was hoping," Roscoe observed dryly, "that you were going to spare us that most overworked of all Latin clichés."

"Not bloody likely," she shot back pleasantly, preempting one of his favorite phrases.

"I liked hockey best, I think," cut in Pete. "The river . . . the black ice . . ." and his memory drifted to the Devon River in frigid midwinter, its swath of ice curving through the stripped bordering woods, the shiny ice black; he visualized days when all the players were out energetically clearing the ice after a snowstorm, the winter winds sometimes howling down the river from the far north country like some call of the ultimate wilderness; the punishing practice sessions, the bump and hurtle and near mayhem, the fatigue of total effort in air seemingly too cold and thin to breathe. He'd loved that, and the bruises and the pains and the chipped front tooth as well.

It had all been violent, but it had not been serious.

After a pleasant half-hour, Pete said, getting up, "I'd better get back and finish unpacking."

"Do come to supper later this week," said Deborah, "any night that suits you. We don't want you to get too lonely . . . a bachelor . . ."

He took his leave, and went out and across the entrance hall to his quarters. A bachelor, that's what he was again, his marriage a false start. He had always detested false starts. Pete could think of nothing else in his life which had been one.

• • •

That night might have been as good as any to accept their invitation to supper—a pleasant hour with "Roscoe" and "Deborah" and would he ever get really used to calling those two icons those two names— but joining them tonight might seem too hurried, as though the hounds of bachelor loneliness were indeed at his heels. The school dining halls would not open until the following day, so that left him with two places to dine in the town of Devon, the Devon Inn, pure preparatory-school gentility, and the townie bar and glorified diner. He chose the latter.

The little bar attached to the dining room there was darker than dim. It was more like a black hole with a few points of light. Very possibly the local drinkers and the occasional fugitive from the school

like himself were not anxious to be seen here. Or
perhaps the murkiness was merely due to thrifty
Yankee minimizing of the electricity bill.

Pete groped his way to an empty stool at the far
end of the bar and from a singularly plain barmaid
ordered Scotch. Was it true that the basic raw material of femininity in New England was simply plainer
than elsewhere? Perhaps because of the rugged winters? Vestigial Puritanism? Poor nutrition? Basic
cussedness?

"You want water with that?" she asked, looking
past his ear.

"No," he answered her emphatically.

There was no doubt that he was even more drawn
to pretty, attractive and beautiful women than other
men seemed to be. It was superficial of him, he
supposed, immature. He should take their *character*
more into consideration. Had he done that, gotten
past the dazzling surface presence of Joan, he might
never have married her. But to ask that kind of
perspicacity or maturity or whatever it was of himself, he realized ruefully, was like asking himself to
become a vegetarian. It just wasn't in the genes.

He ordered, and "ordered" was the word, a second Scotch. The sallow, long-faced barmaid eyed
him sourly as she poured it. Honey, he wanted to
say to her, you don't like me. Do you know something? I don't give a sh—, a damn. Must get those
GI obscenities out of my mind. Government Issue,
from combat boots to cusswords, was suddenly and
exhilaratingly out of date, on the junk heap.

He sipped the Scotch and realized that at some
point in the abrasiveness of war his youthful eager-
ness to please, to be popular, had been almost totally
scraped away. Perhaps he had cared too much, once,
here at Devon as a student for instance, and this
urge by its very intensity had finally been burned
out of him. He certainly had wanted the other guys

here, and the Masters too, to like him, and he certainly had succeeded at that. Having three brothers to learn from as he was growing up hadn't hurt. He had been popular, very popular. And so what? Captain of this team, president of that club: what possible good had it done him or could it do him? He wasn't going to go into politics. It was demeaning to scrape affection from virtually everyone you encountered. *That* was immature.

The dull, vague ache from his leg drifted away on the Scotch for a while. He hardly was aware of it anymore, it was part of him, like his teeth, and for most of the time he was as unaware of the one as of the other. If all trace of pain should disappear from his leg, he would almost miss it; that dull ache was his souvenir, his talisman of four years of his life, his most intense, awful, vivid and grueling ordeal. The ache was really the only palpable thing left to him from the entire war.

"You wanna eat?" the barmaid asked flatly. "Dining room's gonna close."

He paid her and went into the somewhat less murky dining room for one of New England's unremarkable meals. Still, it was bound to beat the Army.

At the table he ordered his third Scotch. This was a special night; he was kind of celebrating. Halfway through the drink, waiting for his steak and boiled potatoes, he suddenly thought: There won't be another war, not another world war. There can't be. There is the atomic bomb now. There is radioactivity. These kids at school here now will never go through what we went through. The UNO will be better than the League of Nations. There will be no armies like those of World War II, no tens of millions of mobilized men, throwing every sophisticated weapon ever invented at each other, and at the civilians in between. We are the last to have to pass

through that. It will never happen again. It won't
because it can't.

Monte Cassino Abbey, one of the great sanctuar-
ies of European culture, pulverized by American
bombers as he watched . . . dead children lying
beside a road . . . skeletal, haunted wraiths in the
prison camp . . . Corporal Bergland's head abruptly
transformed into a kind of bloody mush . . .

• • • •

Two days later, on the opening day of classes, Pete
met with his twelve students in American History.
Even though he was rather underqualified for a
teacher at Devon, holding only a B.A. in the subject,
and was aware an exception had probably been made
for him in this appointment, he felt equal to dealing
with the situation.

For one thing, the physical arrangements for meeting classes at Devon were congenial to him. Teacher
and students sat around an oval table and together
dealt with the subject. He did not have to act like
Moses handing down the law from Mount Sinai to
them. They were meeting, almost conferring, together
and on the same level. He thought back to one or
two grossly inadequate teachers he had himself had
in college, lecturers who from the remoteness of
their position on the podium got away, academically
speaking, with murder, droning pedantic bores who
failed completely to reach their isolated and helpless
students. He was resolved that, whatever else might
happen, he was not going to be that kind of teacher.
In this sunny classroom in Stephens Hall, in wooden
armchairs around this mahogany table, they would
deal with American History and, he was confident,
something would get learned.

The students, dressed as he was in jackets and
ties, filed in rather self-consciously this first day. All
were aware that Mr. Hallam had been some kind of
top athlete and sort of a war hero too.

One tall, somehow weary student sauntered to the seat at the far end of the table, directly opposite Pete's, and sat down with an air of deliberation and a certain attitude of impatience or restiveness, as though he suspected that this course was not really going to be up to his intellectual standards. This precociously jaded personage, Pete later learned from calling the roll, was "Wexford." Beside him sat "Perkins," who seemed to be a pilot fish unable to navigate without the formidable presence of Wexford. Perkins had on an unusual green linen suit which cast a greenish shade over the pallor of his wide fat face. Every few seconds he seemed to check Wexford's face to see if everything was all right.

Next to Perkins a rigid, blond, blue-eyed young man sat down, very lean, with a sharp-cut face and head and a disdainful manner: this turned out to be "Hochschwender."

Three students came in and sat down on the opposite side of the table. One of them Pete already knew about, Cotty Donaldson, because he was captain of the football team and president of the senior class, a good-looking, blondish, broad-shouldered athlete with the kind of pleasant, easy, laughing attitude winners so often had, while they were young, and still winners.

A few others trailed in and then, arriving last, having clearly run some distance, there blew into the room an energetic-looking kid with lively brown eyes, probably rather bright, whom the roll call revealed to be "N. Blackburn," there being a "T. Blackburn" elsewhere in the school.

When they were all seated and had grown expectantly quiet, Pete looked around the table at them and said, "I'm Pete Hallam and you can call me 'Mr. Hallam' or else 'Pete' if you feel like it. But when you're not using my name, you should call me 'sir' because that's still the custom around here."

They were eyeing him, directly or surreptitiously, with an analytical anticipation and suspension of judgment. During the first class or two they would probably accept him or reject him, and the success of the course depended to a certain extent on these first impressions, but Pete knew it to be one of the few compensations for that walk from one end of Italy to the other with people shooting at him that the good opinion of a bunch of adolescent students didn't matter, not at all. He meant to do his best; he thought he could teach them something. Whether they would "like" him, whether he would be "popular," were questions of such lack of importance that in a quiet way he was amused by these noncommittal youngsters as they sat there so alertly, so evidently making up their minds about him.

Then N. Blackburn broke the silence. "Sir," he burst out, "will this course bring us all the way down to World War Two?" and Pete saw that this was some kind of buried compliment and that they were probably going to like him. Presumably that would make the whole process of being a preparatory-school teacher easier. He was not, on the other hand, equipped to deal with "hero worship" from any of them. There were not, he knew in his guts and in his brain, any heroes.

"No, we won't come down to material that recent. I guess you've all been reading the papers and seeing the newsreels these last years. Besides," he heard himself add in a mutter, "we don't know what it meant yet."

There was a rather peculiar silence and then Pete cleared his throat and said, "Let's begin by talking in a general way about the whole subject of American History. I'd like to know what you think of the subject and what your view of American History is, before we start studying it. Um," he looked down at his list of students, "Blackburn," since Blackburn seemed most inclined to speak out.

"Well, sir, I come from a border state. Maryland? That puts people like me in a kind of a funny position when it comes to the Civil War. Some people in my family won't even let me call it that. They say it ought to be called the War Between the States, or even the War for Southern Independence! But, ah, my overall view of American History is, well, let's see, I'd say it's one long success story!"

This was greeted by a distinct snort of disgust from down the table. Its source was the blond, severe-looking boy. Pete consulted his list for the name.

"Well, Hochschwender, what's your view on the subject?"

"I don't know," the student began in a clear, almost metallic voice, as though broadcasting, "whether you will want to hear it. It's a . . . *minority* view," he finished sardonically.

"This is a school," said Pete in his level voice. "All views can be expressed and considered here. We're not indoctrinating you."

"Yes, well," Hochschwender replied coolly, "that's a matter of point of view."

"About your concept of American History," Pete prompted.

"American History," repeated Hochschwender, determined blue eyes rolling up to the ceiling. "Well, American History is just the sum of what the American people make it, that's obvious to anyone. When you get a country like this, made up of the decayed remnants of the aborigines, and then add—"

"You mean the American Indians," interrupted Pete, eyeing him.

"That's right," replied Hochschwender condescendingly, as though it were possible that what he was saying might turn out to be over this teacher's head. "Do you want me to go on?" he inquired.

"Go on."

"Mix the decayed remnants of the aborigines with a lot of flotsam from England, religious fanatics here in New England, bankrupt aristocrats and indentured servants in the South, then add new floods of rejects from Europe, the dregs of inferior places like Ireland and Italy and the Slav countries, pour on a few million savages from Africa, and what do you expect? A mongrel country getting bigger and bigger and winning wars because the land they've got is so rich in resources that they can defeat superior countries."

The startled and angry silence that followed this onslaught was broken by the wayward worldling sitting two seats away from him: Wexford.

"Mr.—ah—what did you say his name is?" he asked Pete.

"That's Hochschwender."

"Mr.—ah—Hochschwender," began Wexford, managing to pronounce the name as though he was gargling a particularly disagreeable mouthwash, "I take it you get your views from *Mein Kampf*?"

Hochschwender fixed his blue eyes on Pete. "What did you say his name is?"

Pete was already regretting throwing the class open to discussion so soon, but he felt he had to go on. "That's Wexford. This school isn't *that* big," he added, trying to reduce the crackling hostility. "Why don't you guys know one another?"

"Some people," answered Hochschwender, "I manage to avoid knowing. Wexford. What kind of name is that? English?"

"Wexford is Anglo-Irish," the other replied. "Irish. As in 'Irish temper.' "

Wexford's face momentarily acquired an odd flush; his mouth set into a peculiar curved line.

Pete said: "Cut out this sniping and these racial cracks. This is a school and all opinions can be expressed, but when they're *that* discredited they won't be allowed to stand. Your view of American History is special, all right, Hochschwender. Someday show me what you've been reading. I'll have some alternative recommendations for you. We'll see if we can't modify the way you look at things during this course. Donaldson?"

The football captain hiked himself forward on his elbows. "Well, sir, can I just say first that the description of this country we've just heard is a bunch of Fascist crap!" He shook his head. "Sorry. Had to say something."

"What's your view of our history?" Pete asked.

"I kind of agree with Nick . . . with Blackburn. I think it's mainly a success with failures here and there. . . . Did we have to have a Civil War to get rid of slavery? That was a failure. Getting slaves in here in the first place. That was another failure. The way we kind of destroyed the American Indian. Couldn't we have incorporated them more into society? But mainly it's been the greatest success in world history, and enterprising people from Europe who were getting strangled by the life in places like Germany came here and got their chance. We had democracy, right from the start. We have a higher standard of living. Our press is free. And uh sir, the American people, well, we don't always take ourselves so seriously, we've got a sense of humor, there's some *fun* here, when there isn't a war on anyway, and we're, we try to be, we do our best to be in spite of having a hard time doing it with some impossible people, we're tolerant." One slicing glance at Hochschwender and Cotty Donaldson was silent.

Hochschwender's hand went up.

"Well?" said Pete.

"Sir," he began in his condescending tone, "since everybody seems to want to attack me and what I said, may I say one more thing?"

Reluctantly Pete replied, "What is it?"

"Sir, this person here, I forget what you said his name was, Wexwell? He's the editor of the school paper, I do know that about him. People have been talking about all the freedom in this country, free press and all. But the paper here isn't just slanted and biased, it's plain stupid. It's an illiterate paper."

The class already despised Hochschwender; even so, they were always and irrevocably ready for a laugh, especially at somebody else's expense. There were suppressed titters of amusement here and there around the table. "It was like that last spring term when Mr. Wearwell took over as editor, and it will be the same thing again this fall."

"Better Wearwell than Werewolf," said Wexford in a challenging undertone.

"Isn't there some way an editor can be replaced?" Hochschwender went on. "Impeachment? Recall? This is a democracy here, as everybody keeps insisting. Can't we have a plebiscite? Can't we vote on keeping Waxwork here or replacing him?"

Two students exploded in mirth. Others were close to it.

Wexford's face, flushed, was totally immobile as he stared in front of him. Perkins, by his side, glanced quickly and apprehensively at him several times, interspersed by alarmed glances around the room.

"Parker," Pete cut in, "how do you see American History from the standpoint of total ignorance you all have at the outset of this course?" Perhaps diverting some slight derision onto Parker would ease the atmosphere.

"I, as a matter of fact"—Parker had been a wrong choice; his eyes were dancing mischievously—"think the key to our history has been the press. Sometimes it's been good and sometimes it's been bad. Sir, do you think editors ought to be chosen by universal suffrage? Universal male suffrage, of course," he finished, barely able to get the words out through suppressed laughter.

Before the class collapsed into a shambles of ridicule of Waxford—*Wexford*—Pete began in his most sober manner to outline the general structure of the course. He'd forgotten just how swiftly this age-group of bright kids could escalate into mockery. Wexford's face was a study in contained—contained *something*—rage? vengefulness? mortification? scorn? Pete didn't like the look. This class was going to take some handling.

The ten o'clock bell sounded. As the students filed out Wexford and Perkins brought up the rear.

"I didn't think that was a bit funny," Perkins ventured, as they went out into the hall.

"Oh, they were funny, in a way. And I'm going to be funny too, now," Wexford said curtly. "Very funny."

•   •   •

Pete had had since his own student days a clear sense of just how that compass of school life, popularity, functioned at Devon.

Cotty Donaldson and the Blackburn boy were clearly very popular, friends of anyone they wanted to befriend, at ease with themselves and each other.

Hochschwender was so special that he was nonexistent in the magnetic field of popularity, but he seemed to be the type of student, probably scientifically minded, who was genuinely and totally indifferent as to how others felt toward him.

Wexford was the interesting betwixt-and-between case. As editor of *The Devonian* he had to have a certain prestige. But he clearly lacked the easy touch, the everyday manner, the effortless gift for camaraderie which made for popularity. The other students accorded him a certain respect but, as had been demonstrated in the first class, this thin surface could

crack in an instant and Wexford be left exposed to
callous, high-spirited derision. He was not exactly
unpopular but he was not important. He didn't really
matter. He was as special as Hochschwender, but he
was not indifferent, not impervious to what others
thought of him. He cared deeply for his prestige, if
not his popularity, and the other students weren't
particularly interested in it or in him. He was a
thwarted boy.

This school, perhaps all schools, consisted in a
series of parades. Some, like Cotty Donaldson's, were
resplendent processions, applauded all the way; others, Hochschwender's, were solitary hikes to which
hardly anyone gave more than one dismissing glance.
Wexford's, self-consciously cheered by Perkins and
perhaps a few others, made its ambiguous way past
torpid spectators. But everyone, every single student,
had to form, if only by himself, some sort of parade
past all of the others, who gave at least one alert
glance to detect any failure, each chink of vulnerabil-
ity. Very occasionally and grudgingly, they might
find something to admire in someone other than the
lords of creation such as Donaldson.

•   •   •

Nick Blackburn that afternoon at five went to Pembroke House to see his brother, Tug. Neither smoked
but they nevertheless met in the semigrubby con-
fines of the Butt Room, the one place in the house
where smoking was legal. Since Pete Hallam was
Nick's History teacher and Tug's faculty adviser,
they had both met this interesting new Master.

"I think he's okay," conceded Tug. This, coming
from one of The Boys in Pembroke House, consti-
tuted high praise.

Unlike his lively, wiry brother, Tug Blackburn was
solid, built for football and heavyweight wrestling.
For him good was good and bad was bad. Occasion-

ally he found his brother too complicated, unnecessarily analytical. Tug felt that if only he told the truth and everyone else told the truth then life would be simple and happy for everyone. Sandy-haired and dark-eyed like his brother, he had the kind of wider, strong face that looked resistable to if not impervious to being punched. The bones looked very hard to break. He had never been punched in anger. He did not believe in anger.

"What'd you do this afternoon?" asked Nick.

"After football practice I gave out some keys—you know, for the Devon Council—keys to some guys who want to practice the piano in the basement of the Chapel after hours, and one to that strange guy in your History class. Hochschwender? He got a key to the little boathouse above the dam. Keeps a single scull in there to work out with on the river. He's got a heart murmur or something. Needs special exercise."

"Why aren't I on the Devon Council?" inquired Nick in half-mocking chagrin.

"Because you're not a sterling character, like me. What is it they say we're supposed to be? 'Representatives of the finest traditions of Devon'? Something like that."

"What you all are is a bunch of dumb athletes who've sucked up to the Masters."

"Somebody has to do stupid chores like handing out those keys, things that are too menial for even the newest Master to bother with. So they name us to the Devon Council and say we represent the finest traditions and all that bull. We get to have dinner at the Devon Inn next May with the Headmaster. And that's it. Whew, what an honor!"

"Man am I impressed."

"Are you puce with envy?"

"Lurid purple."

"Say," said Tug, frowning a little at him. "Isn't it

funny to be starting our senior year and at the end of it, unlike every senior class here in I don't know how many years, no war to be thrown into? Isn't that weird? Until now, you graduated from Devon and you went into the war. I can't even remember much about what it was like before that was the way it went. Can you?"

"No."

"It's really weird. What do we do after we graduate?"

"College of course."

"Yes, but what do we do? I mean, what's the overall aim? No Germany to defeat, no Japan. I don't know: what do we do?"

2

One dark day in late October Nick Blackburn mounted the spiral staircase in the library to the small Readers' Retreat Room, about twenty feet square, long shelves crowding the wall-space with volumes of every size, shape and degree of importance, upward toward the ceiling and a big, foggy-looking skylight.

Wexford was slouched in an easy chair in the corner, poring over a massive volume. He looked up, nodded briefly, and immersed himself again in the book.

The word "slippery" popped into Nick's mind as he covertly studied Wexford's head, hair, hunched shoulders, long hands. The hair was reddish brown and rather long for Devon, almost an affectation, as though Wexford saw himself as Maestro of some symphony. He had a straight nose, slightly sloping hazel eyes, remnants of freckles on his rather long face. His shoulders were tense, despite his slouch; there were, as always, nicotine stains on his long right hand.

"I'm glad you aren't some creep coming up here," Wexford said. "I can't concentrate with creeps around." His voice was mellifluous, urbane, almost pedantic; Nick felt it was an appropriate accompaniment to his somehow singular appearance, a reinforcement of it; there was a languor to his voice and his movements and whole demeanor which, Nick suddenly concluded, was designed to mislead, the steely languor of a cat creeping up on an unaware bird.

Nick searched the shelves as the librarian had directed and, finding his book, settled into a deep, shabby, leather armchair in the corner diagonally across from Wexford's. In the filtered light from the roof he began to read:

A throng of bearded men, in sad-colored garments, and gray, steeple-crowned hats, intermixed with women, some wearing hoods and others bare-headed, were assembled in front of a wooden edifice, the door of which was heavily timbered with oak, and studded with iron pikes.

"What are you reading?" Wexford drawled from across the room.

"Hawthorne, *The Scarlet Letter.*"

Wexford gazed quietly at him.

"Assignment," Nick added, as though it was necessary to make clear he was not reading the story on his own. Why had he felt that? Something about Wexford had made him feel uneasy, even somehow a little defensive.

"New England guilt," sighed Wexford. "Everybody so scared of *sex!*"

"Uh-huh," said Nick in apparent agreement. Now to get off the subject: "What's that tome *you're* buried in?"

"This?"

No, the book on the top shelf, growled Nick to himself.

"This," continued Wexford slowly, "is *The Autobiography of Benvenuto Cellini.* Loads of fun." He looked down at it and then looked up again. "*Not* an assignment," he added with a sly grin.

They relapsed into silence and their books.

Nick soon became engrossed in his story and virtually forgot where he was, who was there with him. The wind sighed around this tower room, rose briefly to a howl, subsided into a sigh again. Nothing suited *The Scarlet Letter* better than this morose New England weather. It was as though spring were never to come, that all of them here in New Hampshire must inhabit these baleful, cheerless days of fall forever, because of their sins, probably.

Across the high, still room Wexford basked in sunny Italy, among the Popes and Medicis, with his gifted scamp, Benvenuto Cellini.

The afternoon lengthened. The wind rose and fell, the skylight darkened. Finally, distantly, the bell of the First Academy Building began its calm, unarguable tolling of six o'clock.

"Dinner," said Nick, getting up.

"Yeah. After dinner let's meet in the Butt Room in the dorm. Something I want to talk to you about. Never see you there. You don't smoke, do you?"

"Um no, I don't," replied Nick.

"It's your lungs, isn't it? Can't smoke."

"Well . . . yes, and no. I had a spot on my lungs once, a long time ago. Now I can forget about it. That's how I missed a year in school and Tug caught up with me. But cigarettes, 'smokes' as they call 'em down home, it doesn't go with sports, does it?"

"I didn't know you were that much of an athlete," said Wexford appraisingly.

"I'm not. Lacrosse, but *JV* lacrosse. The thing is, I like it. I don't play too well, but better than with smokes."

"I'm a damn smokestack myself," said Wexford cheerfully. "Do you think I'm an addictive type of person?"

"Huh?"

"You know, predisposed to get addicted to things, almost anything, nicotine, alcohol, opium, anything.

I drink like a damn fish on vacations. I hear there's a guy in town sells liquor to students."

"I never heard that."

"Aw Nicholas, people don't tell things like that to *you*. They know you're too good."

Screw you, reflected Nick.

But if Nick was supposed to be so good, Wexford, he thought, carried about with him a faint but pervasive aura of delinquency, of being, well, slippery, someone who was as though on a slope, unsteady of foot there, capable of sliding at any moment down into Big Trouble. Nick did not know what had put Wexford in this precarious situation, and he did not know what the Big Trouble might turn out to be, but he sensed this precariousness, this one-false-step away from some abyss.

The dining hall, full of students in jackets and ties huddled around their tables, all seemingly talking at once, the Masters and their wives and children at circular tables in the four corners, isolating themselves as much as possible from this horde of teenage boys filling the rest of the room.

Nick slid into his chair. The five students were already at the table talking about President Truman.

"Who the hell ever said a Midwesterner could be President?"

"Abraham *Lincoln*!"

"He was a Southerner. Kentucky."

"Illinois, you ass."

"Besides, what kind of record did he make? Started the Civil War and then got shot."

"His son was a student here during the Civil War, did you know that?"

"Is that right? Well, so what?"

"Truman doesn't *look* like a President and doesn't *sound* like a President—"

"Whoever heard what any President but Roosevelt *sounded* like? Who the hell knows what Herbert Hoover sounded like?"

"Truman's a small kind of man. That's what we need now that the war's over. What next? We're not going to have any more wars—"

"Are *you* kidding! Wait'll the Russians get the atom bomb."

"—As I was saying before being so rudely interrupted by that Red Baiter over there, we're not going to have any more wars but we *are* going to have another Depression of course, and Truman's just the man for that. After all, he was a failure wasn't he, didn't he go bankrupt or something?"

"He plays a nice piano."

"What do you guys know about it, anyway? Buried up here in the sticks. What the hell do you know about high politics?"

"Oh drop dead, we read the papers don't we, hear the news?"

"My father *is* in the Cabinet."

There was a semirespectful silence as everyone recalled this fact, then someone said, "All right, what does he say about Truman?"

"He doesn't say anything. But *I* think he thinks he's okay."

Nick said, "We're all going to kind of miss Roosevelt. My father wasn't in the Cabinet or anything, but he sure did have opinions about Roosevelt. He said he was a traitor and a Communist and a labor agitator and a spendthrift ruining the free-enterprise system, and that he was insane. I took it all in, and then I'd hear him on the radio or see him in the newsreel and think, There he is, our President, taking care of the country. Made me feel kind of secure, having this insane Communist traitor taking care of the country."

The others laughed, rather in spite of themselves; no one at Devon was especially anxious to pay such a tribute to anyone else: tribute from your peers was the rarest commodity in the school.

The argumentative, semihostile atmosphere dissipated. Nick felt a little relieved to notice this. There was a violence lying around, like unexploded shells, hand grenades which anybody in a rage might blindly hurl, left over from the incredibly abrupt end of the war, just last August.

After dinner he crossed the dark campus in the chill evening air, past windows with light streaming from them as students settled in for a night of study, went into his dormitory and down the stairs to the Butt Room, which was empty except for Wexford.

There the only legal radio available to the students in the dormitory was broadcasting the seven o'clock news. As Wexford motioned him to a broken chair next to his own broken chair, Nick heard snatches of the news items over the hubbub of smoking and talking students: "Eleanor Roosevelt, the late President's widow . . . called to her hotel window during a visit to London . . . GIs in the street below demanded to know why there was transportation home for British war brides and not for them. . . . In Manila, American soldiers demanding repatriation were rioting. . . . In Paris . . ."

All around the globe, one outcry from all the millions of scattered Americans: Home!

"Curious feeling," Wexford remarked, "missing the great drama *de nos jours* just by a hair, by being one year too young. I guess we'll always be sort of a new Lost Generation because of that."

"Think so? We're all going to run wild and get drunk and dance on tabletops, like the twenties?"

"Maybe not," said Wexford, his eyes concentrating. "There *is* something left for us, people our age, to do for the country."

"Oh yeah? What's that?"

Wexford looked at him and then looked away.

"All the important countries of the world were cleansed by this war, you know, except us."

"Cleansed?"

"I don't really have to spell it out for you, do I?" He looked at him. "Yes, I see I do. It's so simple. Suffering purifies, everybody knows that, artists suffering in garrets to get inspiration, saints fasting in the desert, monks flagellating themselves—"

"Doing *what*?"

"I'm not getting sexy. *Beating* themselves." He cocked an eye at him. "Unless you call *that* sexy."

"Are you crazy?"

"No, I guess you don't. What I'm talking about has been called 'the dark night of the soul.' Suffering. That's how people are purified. John the Baptist in the Desert. Christ in Gethsemane. The Jews during their Captivity. You see, it happens to whole people too, nations, not just individuals."

"Wexford, I'm afraid I don't get you."

For just a split second Wexford's long face set in an expression of impatience. It made his usually animated features look suddenly bleak, even almost old. There was in fact something ageless about his face, something fortyish in it now, as there would be something boyish in it at forty. A changeling among the generations.

Now his face lit up again and he began patiently, his slightly unctuous, rather deep—almost affectedly deep, as though compensating for innate shrillness—voice growing confidential: "Look what's happened in the last fifteen years to every important country—that is, *except* the United States of America. Japan invades China in 1931, and there was nothing but war and starvation and hell on earth in that country from that day until last August. France gets completely overrun and occupied by its worst enemy, Germany, and has its face ground into the mud by the Nazis; the French people had the Gestapo at their throats; in other words, wiped out in the Pride department. England? The Germans bomb the bejesus out of England, the country gets stripped bare, like Mother Hubbard's cupboard, trying to fight and pay for another huge war. The British Empire? Forget about that, that's all over, the Recessional is playing. Bit the dust, the British have, in the Great Nation department. Russia? Scorched earth all over the place, the whole country a wreckage, who knows how many millions dead, a wreck. Italy? *We* took care of that, ravaged Italy from the tip of the boot to the Alps, blasted the hell out of Naples, wrecked Cassino, left the Italians starving and ruined, took away their Empire. I believe St. Peter's is intact. We let the Colosseum go on being the ruin it already was. They've still got the Ponte Vecchio. Getting older every day. The Leaning Tower hasn't gone all the way yet. Otherwise, Italy is done for. Germany? We bombed the unholy daylights out of every damn city they've got, the Russians overran the East and we overran the West and Germany is one living hell and wreck. Take Japan. Same story, with the added holocaust of two atomic bombs laid on them, just for good measure." He paused and pulled deeply on his cigarette: an actor, too, Nick noticed. "And that leaves the U.S. of A. One spent Japanese torpedo drifted up on one California beach, and that's the only shot fired in anger against the continental United States during the worst war in history. One spent shell. We're untouched. We've been spared the baptism of fire. And so there's no redemption. We haven't been saved. We're still in danger."

"No baptism of fire? What do you call Pearl Harbor, losing the Philippines? What about all the hundreds of thousands of guys who got killed in—"

"Exactly. In Guadalcanal, in Italy, in North Africa, in the Pacific somewhere, in France. But no men got killed by the enemy, not one, on United States soil.

Not one American civilian was killed or injured.
There was no damage to any property on our soil.
We never were scared, not in our streets we weren't.
They never got here. Do you realize what that saved
the American psyche from? Think how we would
have felt if we'd seen Germans parading down Fifth
Avenue in New York, locking up President Roosevelt, pasting up orders on buildings telling what
time we had to be home, what we couldn't read,
how much we'd be allowed to eat, if anything, how
many thousand people were going to be hauled away
to Germany as slave labor? Suppose they'd come up
here a year or so ago and told us to get into uniform
and drill, threw out half our textbooks, told us what
not to read, carted away a dozen teachers and fifty
students to God knows where? What if you'd seen
your house blow up, with your mother inside, and
your baby sister, and your little dog?"

"We have been lucky in a way."

"Bismarck said, 'God takes special care of drunks
and America.' But the thing about it is, good luck is
bad luck." He gazed at Nick expectantly.

Nick thought: This guy has more bullshit than a
snake-oil salesman. And why is he throwing it all at
me? Aloud, he said, "I don't get you, Wexford. That's
a little too fancy or something for me. 'Good luck is
bad luck.' Whaaaat?"

"Listen, Nicholas, don't pull back into your I'm-just-
a-simple-minded-young-athlete routine. I'm talking
to you like this because I know you've got the brain
to comprehend it. You're saying to yourself that
what I'm telling you is bullshit because that's what
your brother Doug or Thug or whatever his name is
would say."

I *know* that's what Tug would say, reflected Nick.

"You had that bad lung, maybe you thought you
were going to die at one time. So, *you* have been

cleansed. You're like China," he concluded, blinking expectantly at him.

Oh my God, sighed Nick inwardly. If only Tug were here. As it was, facing this alone, Nick's defenses were imperfect, and some inkling of what Wexford was driving at forced itself into his consciousness.

"I'm saying something very simple: it's this: the U.S. of A. is still full of poisons because we weren't defeated or occupied or even bombed in the war. So we've got all the crust of selfishness on us, we're greedy, hypocrites, *lechers*, because our vices didn't get bled and scraped and blasted away by the war."

"What should we do," Nick inquired in a not-bad imitation of Wexford's own dry drawl, "attack Russia?"

"Keep an eye out," Wexford replied with a serious wink, "just keep an eye out."

"Wexford," said Nick, staring into his greenish, slightly sloping eyes, "there's something . . . ah . . . *Hochschwenderish* in these theories of yours."

"Blackburn," Wexford replied, "every serious thinker like me discovers sooner or later that there's some crackpot somewhere who's spouting a kind of dizzy parody of what we're teaching."

"You're a theorist? You're a teacher? Gee, if you don't mind my saying so, you sure do take yourself seriously."

Wexford stared at the opposite wall. "Yes," he said.

•   •   •

The next day Indian Summer arrived in New Hampshire, sweeping the Arctic air back into Canada for a brief while, hustling the lowering gray clouds away, and revealing a pure blue sky, with washed northern sunshine lighting the brilliant autumn trees. There was a strongly northern near-the-top-of-the-world clearness in the skies, an edge to the wind, more beautiful because so fleeting, up there close to the great northern wilderness.

On the campus this sudden remission in the weather stirred up a feeling of recklessness, an urgent uneasiness.

Peter Hallam was helping out that day with varsity football practice in the stadium in the Fields Beyond. As the boys went through their fairly grueling warm-up routines Pete noticed that Tug Blackburn and Cotty Donaldson, Pembroke House roommates, were, as directed, slamming into each other, shoulder pad against shoulder pad, with hearty good humor.

"Is that the best you can do?" . . . "Any harder and I'd"—slam—"break that little collarbone of yours." . . . "Why doesn't your *brother* put himself" —slam—"through this? Chicken?" . . . "No. Intelligent." . . . "You mean"—*slam*—"I'm not?" . . . "Of"—*slam*—"course not! It's just that"—*slam*—"you hide it under your"—*SLAM*—"shoulder pads!"

Then they ran some plays. There was a battering scrimmage.

Afterward, in the failing light, Tug and Cotty walked back across the wide sweep of fields with Pete.

"How'd you decide to come back here and teach, Pete?" asked Cotty. "Didn't you—well, with the outside world and all, business or well *government*, didn't something like that attract you more? Devon, here . . ."

Pete understood the unexpressed sentiment Cotty was fumbling with; Devon, while okay for students, in fact one of the two best preparatory schools in the country, seemed a real dead-end backwater for a Master. Pete had felt the same way when he had been a student here.

"Or if you wanted to teach," put in Tug, "wouldn't

you want to go on to Harvard, or you were Dartmouth, weren't you? Dartmouth?"

"I like it here." Pete did not know how to analyze
better the complex and deep reasons, probably only
half-understood even by himself, that had made him
step unhesitatingly into this opportunity when it
appeared. Before Italy he would never have considered it. Pete Hallam, a prep-school teacher? He had
seen himself, dimly it's true, as some kind of leader,
perhaps in business, perhaps in law, possibly government. But he had seen himself out in the world,
as they said.

And yet he had instinctively moved, some might
think retreated, to Devon when the opportunity
occurred.

He had to say more to them than "I like it here."
Obviously they had been discussing him at length
and in depth among themselves. "Why would a
neat guy like that settle for Devon?" . . . "Maybe
it's just a stepping-stone to something better." . . .
"Yeah, but *what*?" He remembered such discussions
about certain Masters himself.

"The kind of war I was in," he began unwillingly,
but began nevertheless, out of a respect for these
kids, "was a mess and a grind of filth and bloodi-
ness from beginning to end. Then I was, you know,
a prisoner. My leg. You've noticed that."

They both nodded.

"So, when they asked me to come up here, well,
Devon isn't a mess, is it? I had to, I guess, catch my
breath." Maybe I'll spend the rest of my life here, he
added to himself, trying to catch my breath. "You
need some perspective after . . . the kind of thing
we had in Italy."

The boys were subliminally elated: Pete had said
something about his war experience.

"Do you think you'll stay on?" ventured Cotty. "I
mean for years?"

"I don't know," Pete shrugged. His future was a blank, featureless wall. He had not, on some profound level, expected to have one.

• • •

The results of that day's overstimulation included a broken leg at football practice, a lacerated skull on the squash courts, and one varsity lacrosse player punched by an assistant coach. Mrs. Wherry, the Headmaster's wife, was carried away by two glasses of sherry into telling the Dean that he was "too spooky" for the younger students. In Mr. Latch's Latin class, the smallest student who, declining *hic, haec, hoc*, gave the accusative case as *huem, huam, huam*, found himself stuffed by the Master into the wastebasket.

At Devon there were just two outlets for energy available to the students: study and sports. Out on the fringes were extracurricular activities and religion, but the two great avenues lying foursquare in the student's path were his books and his team. Students were forbidden to go to the movie house in town. They could listen to a radio only in the Butt Room and only for a short period. They could not leave this isolated New England village without special permission, they were of course not allowed to own any vehicle more sophisticated than a bicycle, any student caught using any alcoholic beverage was immediately expelled, and God only knew what would happen if any sexual experimentation was discovered.

There were no rules at Devon, ran the standard conundrum explaining suitable behavior in the school, until they were broken.

Wexford's Brain Trust met that afternoon in one of the piano practice rooms in the basement of the Chapel. These rooms were soundproof; the thick insulation had not been concealed behind paneling, and the result was walls of a strange-looking white foamlike substance, held in place by metal strips. It was in essence a padded cell.

Wexford sat before a battered baby grand piano and once in a while capriciously strummed the keyboard, playing snatches of "Rustles of Spring," "The Blue Danube Waltz."

The two other students, as he strummed Strauss, were debating the question he had set for them: which student or group of students was the worst menace to the Devon School, the Devon spirit?

"What about Sol Abrahamson?" suggested Billy Carruthers.

"Oh please," responded Wexford, "just because he's Jewish. Don't be so conventional. I don't want clichés. I want *real menaces.*"

"The football squad?" put in Peavy Pierson.

"Hm."

"Well . . ."

"They're *dumb* all right."

"Not all of them are."

"Bullies, sort of, sometimes."

"What about athletes in general?"

"Oh well, after all, that takes in—"

"Lots of show-offs and—"

Wexford brought his hands down grandly on a major chord. All fell silent. "You're all so far off the point I can't believe it. Can't you see? The older guys in the Army defeated the Germans and the Italians and the Japs, but now the war is over. There's no organization left, or soon won't be. Every damn serviceman all over the world wants to get back home and who can blame them and soon nobody will be protecting the U.S. of A. against anything, just as it was before the war. Well, *we* didn't do anything to help with that menace, so I say it's up to us, our generation, the Just-Missed, to contribute something. What? Keep an eye out, that's what, for it happening again!"

"What happening again?" asked Billy Carruthers in a wondering voice.

"Some other group trying to destroy our freedom and our way of life. And let me tell you where that group will come from. Right from inside this country, that's where. Because Americans haven't really been through it, haven't been tested and wrecked, not at home we haven't. Some other group is going to try to take over. Let's just look around our class, around this school."

Peavy Pierson sighed. "I've never noticed anything like that."

"Then let me mention a few people you should notice," said Wexford firmly. "I suggest you notice Eric Hochschwender, and Rob Willis, not to mention Ernie Manero and Gene DelliGatti."

"For one thing," persisted Peavy, "I don't see how Ernie Manero and Eric Hochschwender can be part of some kind of conspiracy against the 'Devon spirit' or 'our way of life' when they hate each other's guts, don't speak, and have had two fistfights at least."

Wexford idly did a trill on the piano, C-E, C-E, C-E. Then he rolled his eyes in Peavy's direction. "Don't you know a feint when you see one? Everybody thought Hitler was getting ready to invade England, so what did he do? He attacked Russia! Standard procedure. If we see the Wops fighting the Krauts around here, we get lulled"—he paused to allow the fineness of the phraseology and the subtlety of the insight to register—"into false complacency." The first bars of the Mendelssohn "Wedding March" came forth from the piano and then he said, "Once they've got us in that frame of mind, why, they can just take control of the class and the school, and the future."

"Just because they're German and Italian by descent, and some of those guys are only partly one or the other," said Billy Carruthers, still smarting slightly from the dismissal of his Abrahamson suggestion, "doesn't mean they're enemies. Heck, *Eisenhower* is German!"

"Ernie Manero's a good guy," said Peavy. "He really is. He's about as much a Fascist as Kate Smith is. And, come to think of it, his father's a Brigadier General or something in the Marine Corps!"

"I didn't say," put in Wexford placatingly, "that the students I named are the real menace. I didn't mean that at all. I'm merely suggesting that we keep an eye on them. Eric Hochschwender is and always has been a Nazi sympathizer and never made any bones about it."

There was an uncomfortable silence.

"Eric donated blood to the Red Cross just last week," said Peavy in half-protest.

C-D, C-D trilled on the piano. "Mm," murmured Wexford.

3

Nick and Tug Blackburn tried to live as separate and distinct lives as two brothers in the same preparatory school could.

Tug was a senior and "an athlete." At Devon, if you attained a certain level of skill and recognition in one or more sports, you were stamped "an athlete" by the collective consciousness and that was that. It was prestigious to be an athlete, provided you were not "a ringer"—that is, a Boston-area high-school graduate recruited and subsidized for one year at Devon, to flesh out the football squad. Ringers were viewed as semirespected outsiders, too special to be in competition for status, and without that, barely existing there.

Tug Blackburn lived with other athletes in the back wing of Pembroke House, which seen from the street appeared to be solidly respectable, concealing a battered collection of exhausted rooms in the wing at the back.

Nick Blackburn lived in somewhat less raucous Saltonstall Hall, a red-brick, ivy-covered dormitory with a commingling of athletes, a couple of class leaders, some good students, and a number of boys ruthlessly classified as "grinds" and "creeps." Here prevailed a general atmosphere of live-and-let-live.

Two Masters and their families inhabited ground-floor apartments and maintained a simmering truce with the students.

Saturday morning at six, the Blackburn brothers and four other skiers stumbled into Pete Hallam's rooms in Pembroke House. All of them had heard through the school grapevine that Pete was prepared to drive them over to Vermont for a weekend on the slopes. The school had no organized ski team: interested boys got to go to the mountains when Pete would take them.

"First time this year! I can't believe it, I can't believe it! We're going skiing!"

"My legs feel like Jell-O."

"You think the slopes will be crowded with a lot of damn snow bunnies?"

"It's too *cold* out for them. They only come out when the conditions are perfect, so they can ruin them."

"I forget how to ski," said Nick ingenuously, half meaning it.

"Just lean forward," said Cotty Donaldson.

"Bend the knees," said R.T.

"Follow Pete," said Chet. "Do what he does."

"*I* can't do what he does," Nick protested.

"Try," ordered Tug flatly.

"Try! And get killed?"

"Then *don't* try to do what he does," advised Tug. "To thine own self be true."

"And it must follow as go the night the day—"

"That thou canst not get to the bottom of the slope!"

The six students and the young Master piled into Pete's station wagon with their equipment, skis in the rack on top. The sun had risen upon an icy world of powder-dry gleaming snow, rigid, frigid white colonial houses beneath the canopy of limitless blue sky. The little town's streets and sidewalks

were buried beneath packed snow and edged by the
mounds of spotless snow thrown up by plow and
shovel. Devon was beautiful, set in its wintry land-
scape as it was built to be, upright and tightly closed
and venerable and enduring.

They proceeded westward along back roads into
ever more thinly settled country, threading into hill
country and then toward the mountains, silent and
almost hostile-seeming masses of half-shrouded gray-
ness, looming and formidable.

Are we supposed to "conquer" these? Nick wondered in wry uneasiness.

"I've never skied this place we're going today,
have you?" he asked Tug, a rather formidable shape
himself in his dark blue parka, heavy knitted cap
and goggles.

"Yup. It's hell. There's a slope there called Suicide
Six. I don't recommend it for you."

"Tell me the name of the one you do recommend,"
said Nick.

"I forget. Mother's Milk or something like that."

"Drop dead."

While Tug was a very good skier, Nick was not so
bad. Privately he classified himself as either the best
intermediate or the worst expert skier in the world.

At the ski area the day's temperature, hovering
around fifteen degrees, with a brisk razory wind
cutting through the mountains, had in fact kept all
but the hardiest skiers away. Grabbing the rope tow
they were hauled to the top of the slope. While what
lay below them could not compare to trails on Mount
Mansfield further north, it was challenging enough,
a steep terrain of bumps and hillocks, exposed rocks,
clumps of evergreen and white birch, icy patches.
With Pete in the lead they proceeded down it single
file, slaloming through the various hazards, careen-
ing into an occasional skidding fall and even one or
two headlong somersaulting wipeouts, taking brief

airborne jumps as they hurtled over the hillocks. The chill, clean air scrubbed off the musty and book-ish webbing of the school; panting and flushed, they pulled up beside the trail for a brief respite, plumes of frosted breath pumping out.

All of this struck Nick as a completely real chal-lenge and even a kind of threat, physical and imme-diate. He had to forget rivalries and petty doubts; small resentments and large anxieties were crowded out. This was real and this was dangerous and this was what life, he thought hurriedly, really ought to be all about.

"How's this for a strange feeling?" Nick said to his brother as they waited in line for the tow. "Now that the war's over I'm beginning to miss it."

"Um-hum."

"While it was going on, I was kind of *scared* of it there for a while."

"Hm."

"The newsreels of guys' bodies facedown in the sand on beaches, waves lapping in and out, making them *move* a little . . . dead bodies moving."

"Mm."

"But now that the damn thing's over I'm begin-ning to—well, we missed something, we missed it. The big drama of the century. We missed getting sent to some strange part of the world and doing some strange thing there, like being a frogman and swimming underwater into Tokyo Harbor and attach-ing a mine to a Jap battleship."

"That the way you saw yourself?"

"Something like that. How did you see yourself?"

"Well, you remember I thought the paratroops would be good."

"That's it, something like that. You stand up in some big transport plane and attach your chute line to the clothesline or whatever it was in the cabin, and you move on up to the door and then by God

you just throw yourself out into space, over *Sicily*
say, and then float down. Where are we ever going
to be able to do things like that now?"

"The guys who were really in it—Pete, some others I've met, prisoners or wounded or both—let me
tell you, they didn't think it was some great adventure. They didn't like it. They hated it. I think they
kind of feel they've been damaged forever by it.
Even if they weren't wounded."

"I know," agreed Nick automatically. He did know.
But he was also sure the war had been a great
adventure, potentially anyway, and they had missed
it.

They reached the head of the line and Nick stepped
forward, locked his left arm around the moving rope
and grasped it behind his back with his right hand.
He was yanked upward, through a grove of pine
trees.

At the top the others were waiting. They started
swiftly down the slope. All were well warmed up
now, and skiing well. No one fell, even though Pete
set a somewhat faster pace. At the bottom Nick
skidded toward a stop, misjudged his speed, and
took Tug, already stopped, broadside. Both collapsed
in a clatter of skis and poles.

"You dumb—"

"I misjudged it."

"You meant to."

"I hit ice."

"I *said* you should have stayed on Mother's Milk!"
They disentangled themselves and struggled to
their feet. "You'll never make an athlete," observed
Tug, readjusting his goggles.

"Who ever said I wanted to be an athlete?"

"What do you want to be?" inquired Tug, grimacing.

"I want to be General Patton. Or General Rommel."

"Would you settle for Sad Sack?"

"You'd know more about that than I would."

They drove back through the icy bluish dusk, crisp banks of snow high on both sides of the narrow country road, to the farmhouse where they would stay overnight.

A fire crackled in the fireplace; there were hooked rugs, plain maple furniture, a low ceiling, small-paned windows excluding the closing-in New England night-time freeze.

At dinner there were plain, copious piles of food which the students seemed to inhale, and afterward they sat around on the floor by the fire, or went into the storage room to repair the wax on their skis.

Nick asked Pete what he thought of the day's skiing.

"Too easy," he remarked with a trace of a grin. "A rope tow! We never used to have anything like that. Tramp up and ski down, that's the way it was. Get your legs loosened up. You were all warmed up—I'll say you were—by the time you'd hiked to the top of one of these slopes and were ready to start down. We didn't have so many injuries, broken legs. Soon there'll be all kinds of tows and lifts and then . . . the sport will be different." He took a poker and turned over a log on the grate. "Everything's going to be different, now that the war's over."

"More fun?"

"Oh you bet, *much* more fun."

Nick thought he heard an edge of irony in this reply. "Better?" he persisted.

Pete cocked a quizzical eye at him.

Later in the Bunk Room Tug climbed into the bottom bunk, Nick in the one above him. "What is this Wexford guy all about?" Tug murmured, as the others in the big room were settling down for the night.

"What do you mean?" asked Nick. "I don't know."

"He says he's a friend of yours."

"Well I wouldn't say that. He—"

"I was in the Weight Room in the gym, doing some extra exercise, and he saunters in—I never spoke to the guy before—says he's a friend of yours. Then he starts asking me about some players on the team."

"Football squad?"

"Yeah. Their 'attitude,' that's what he kept talking about. What kind of 'attitude' did they have? I said, 'Attitude toward what?' and he said, 'Oh, the team, the school, sportsmanship, toward the country.' 'They're for God, for country, and for Devon,' I said. He didn't seem to think it was funny. The point is, it was a weird conversation. First of all, I don't know him. Now you tell me he really isn't a friend of yours. What's he up to?"

"Search me," said Nick a little drowsily.

"I don't like people I don't know snooping around. You know what he said about Ernie Manero? . . . Are you listening?"

"Mm."

"He said, 'I'd watch him if I were you.' I said, 'Why?' and he said, 'Listen, friend, we've got to win the peace.' Listen, *friend*! Win the peace! Is he some kind of nut or what?"

"Oh no," said Nick tiredly. "He's not crazy. But he's got all these theories."

"Guy I don't even know," mused Tug.

• • •

Next morning at six-fifteen Pete called out in a cheerful and authoritative voice, "Everybody up! It's late! Slope's waiting!"

"It's *late*," grumbled someone. "Do you know what time it is? A quarter after *six*!"

"These muscular Christians," agreed another voice.

"I suppose he'll want us to take cold showers next."

Soon they were on the gleaming hillside; a wintry sun emerged from the clouds now and then to evoke a dazzling silvery glare upon the snow. As they traversed and sideslipped, schussed and bumped down the slopes there was a general tacit feeling among the members of the Devon School Unorganized Ski Group that this was as ideal a day, an outing, an escape from the constrictions of school life, as New England could possibly offer.

Toward late afternoon long shadows from the surrounding hills crept across much of the area, and a new chill came into the wind, a harbinger of dusk, of sub-sub-freezing temperatures, of nature turning her coldest shoulder once again.

At the beginning of the last run, at the top of the slope, Nick skied down a short distance and then pulled off to the side. The others shot smartly past him and within moments he was quite alone, at the top of hummocky, plummeting Suicide Six, dusk and shadow and chill rapidly closing in, the sun lost behind the western hills. He had been skiing all day and he was tired, his legs ached, he was sore and a bit bruised from several falls. Far, very far indeed below him he could see the bottom of the rope tow and the parking lot where one of the toylike cars would be Pete's station wagon. The others would soon be reaching it.

A feeling, not exactly of panic, but a cold sense of isolation crept over him. If he happened to fall and twist his knee badly and be unable to ski the rest of the way down, it might be quite some time before anyone got to him . . . and when darkness fell . . .

Cut it out, he said to himself. Get on with it.

He pulled back onto the trail, the snow now a ghostly grayish pall in the icy dusk, and headed downward, checking every few seconds as the slope nose-dived bumpily through the surrounding pines.

What if I catch an edge and go sailing off into the trees?

As he bounced over a hummock his tips crossed;

he poled into the air, straightening them just in time; the next moment he was too far back, out of control; he lurched forward, regaining position. Then he pulled off to the side for a moment, panting, then back onto this impossible slope—how right Tug had been—and toiling like a slave laborer in Nazi Germany, his legs a mass of aches, he at last came in sight of the bottom, and reaching the runout he relaxed, standing upright, poles dangling from outstretched hands, and sailed up to the others, who were waiting for him.

"You're improving," observed Tug.

Nick bent down to undo his release binding, hands shaking. "Think so?"

"Yeah. A little."

In the long, drowsy ride back to Devon, Nick said, "Why isn't school always like this? Now this has been what I'd call an okay school day."

"You mean you don't *like* Latin at eight-ten A.M.?" inquired Cotty.

"Doesn't physics thrill you anymore?" asked Tug.

"All those beautiful hours memorizing French vocabulary, those terrific irregular verbs?" put in R.T.

"Oh me," sighed Nick, "that all starts again tomorrow, doesn't it? Physics. Latin. Chapel. Gym. Prune whip. Lights out. Ugh."

"You could be dead," murmured Pete from behind the wheel.

"On Suicide Six?" began Nick in disbelief. "That wasn't—"

"I didn't mean skiing."

The boys fell silent. Very rare indeed it was when Pete made any allusion at all to the war.

4

Wexford went home to his family's place on Cape Cod that same weekend. He was not a skier and in fact he was not at all athletic. He looked as though he could have been an athlete if he had bothered to take the time—tall, lean, rather rangy, fluid in his movements. The assumption was that he had no time to be on a varsity squad, that his mind teemed with so much intellectual energy, so many theories and projects, that there was little left over for sports.

Some athletic activity being required however every weekday from every student, Wexford chose golf in the autumn. Who knew who was on the golf course? One of his minions could always sign in for him at the clubhouse, leaving him free to read and plan and talk and influence. During the winter term he was officially out for cross-country skiing, which, unlike the Blackburn boys' unorganized downhill team, was officially recognized by the school. With cross-country skiing as with golf, the Physical Education Department was very uncharacteristically a little vague as to just who was where in the woods at what time, and so Wexford was free to strum a grand piano for hours in one of the padded cells in the basement of the Chapel, fold himself into an easy chair in the

Readers' Retreat Room and peruse volumes on the Decline and Fall of the Roman Empire, or the France of Marcel Proust, or Nietzsche. Beside him as he read were invariably a little notebook and a pen, and he wrote down every word he did not know whenever he encountered one, looked up its meaning, and added it to his vocabulary. In the spring term he returned once more to golf, that is, he virtually never saw the golf course but had his name faithfully entered every day.

Once when he deigned actually to play a few holes he encountered the coach. "Well, Wexford, hardly ever see you out. How's that slice of yours?" The coach, part-time, a preoccupied Chemistry teacher, always inquired about everybody's slice.

"Better, much better!" replied Wexford, radiating his widest, warmest grin. "You don't see me so much because I always play the back nine." "Back-Nine Billy" the other golfers called him tolerantly; if he was peculiar enough not to like this great sport, to avoid the epic encounters on the links, so much the worse for him. Wexford was definitely special; he had their respect. They didn't understand him.

Virtually alone among Devon boys Wexford was sallow—a lounge lizard, bookworm, pianist, smoker, palaverer, debater, away-from-school drinker, and rumor had it secret drinker at the school as well.

His parents' third home was in Wellfleet, near the tip of Cape Cod. Their main residence was a fine old town house in Brooklyn Heights, New York, because Mr. Wexford refused to move too far from his roots in a less fashionable part of the borough. They had been coming to their Wellfleet house, war or no war, for many autumn weekends. The second house was in Palm Beach.

That weekend Wexford took the Boston-and-Maine train to Boston and then the bus down to the Cape. Everywhere men in uniform crowded every accom-

modation, facility, aisle, seat, men's room, snack
counter. The whole country seemed in counterflux:
all the enormous energy which had flung millions of
servicemen outward to the war fronts was now revers-
ing itself and they were being sucked back, a vast
reversal tumbling inward upon the startled and
unprepared, though grateful, forty-eight states.
Atabrine-dyed yellow-faced veterans of the Pacific,
drawn-looking survivors of Italy, rotund sailors and
raunchy airmen collided with one another on their
hurried routes homeward.

Cape Cod looked desolation itself in December:
shuttered summer houses, stripped trees, mournful
dunes, gale-braced natives.

His mother met him at the bus station in the old,
prewar Cadillac. She was, if anything, more nervous
than ever, thinner too, the hands on the steering
wheel with their diamonds looking a little like claws.
He noticed she was dyeing her hair a subdued
auburn. Her silver fox jacket looked old, as did the
car, as she did herself. It had been a long war.

In the back seat the eleven-year-old twins, Warren
and Winston, piped up with questions about his
sports accomplishments. So Wexford told them about
hockey, how he was not the captain of the team, no,
only the co-captain, about how they were going to
play St. Paul's in the Boston Garden, and about the
black ice on the Devon River where they practiced.

"I never heard all of this," remarked his mother
abstractedly. "You never write about it. Your letters," she finished in a rather plaintive voice, "are
always so *cerebral.*"

If the boys mentioned this spurious hockey career
of his to his father, an absurd and sticky situation
could result. He would take that chance; Wexford
was always taking chances like that. It was exciting.

The house, a rambling white clapboard structure
with green shutters, looked out over the dunes to

Massachusetts Bay. Wexford dropped his bag and coat in the front hall for one of the maids to put in his room, forgetting that there now was only one overworked and rebellious maid left. He went to the Steinway concert grand piano next to the bay window, and as though serenading the deserted dunes and the gray, wind-whipped water outside, swept into Debussy's "Jardins sous la Pluie." Its technical challenge was too much for him but he faked it with plenty of pedal and flamboyant hands. The twins applauded. They were the only children left at home. Wexford's older brother was still in England with the Army Air Force.

His father, who was always referred to as Father, never Dad or Daddy or (God forbid) Pop, came down presently and he and Wexford repaired to the library for highballs. Father believed in teaching his children to drink at home, and was suspicious of any man who did not drink: "He doesn't trust himself, so why should I trust him?" was his invariable verdict.

"How's that school?" Father asked dubiously.

"So-so," replied Wexford. "The new class is kind of weird-looking. Undersized, I'd say. Maybe it's the war."

"Maybe I should have sent you to Culver."

Wexford inwardly blanched at the thought of the unending hours of dismal drill a military school would have entailed. He said, "At least now some of the younger teachers will be coming back and these senile old codgers can be put back out to pasture."

His father's long, closed face remained in the expression it had held before these words. Wexford noticed this. Wexford noticed everything. One of his father's favorite aversions, the incompetent aged, had undergone a sea change, a time transformation. The old were not to be summarily dismissed anymore.

"Of course old Mr. Patch-Withers in History is as

good as ever," drawled Wexford cheerfully. "Some people are just indestructible, kind of ageless."

Father said, looking him over, "You could use some new clothes, judging from those worn-out gray flannel pants and that jacket you've got on."

"I never think about clothes. Too many—"

"You've got to, now the war's over. Appearances are going to start to matter again."

Later, at dinner, the big window in the dining room black as pitch except where the dining-table candles were reflected in it, the silver, crystal subdued opulence, the twin boys suitably wordless, Wexford said casually, "I'm going to be writing the editorials in *The Devonian* for the rest of the year. Got the other editors to agree. First time they've ever let one editor do them all."

Father looked unimpressed. "Sometimes I think you get all these 'honors' of yours just because you'll do things nobody else wants to do."

Wexford knew that this was true. Shrewd Father had put his finger on it as usual. But what Father did not take into account was that by doing the drudgery Wexford was gaining influence, power.

"Most of the students there," he said, "don't know *what* they think. You tell 'em, they'll think it. I plan to tell 'em."

"Tell them what, for example?" Father inquired.

"Well, for one thing, defend our traditions against foreign influences: Fascism, Communism."

"Anglicanism?" inquired Father dryly. The Wexfords were prominent Episcopalians.

Wexford came as close to a sheepish grin as he could manage.

"I mean all the latest rotten European 'isms.' Got to be guarded against."

Father's fixed sternness relaxed somewhat. "Well, to be serious, you're right. And the most potent European 'ism' to be guarded against is of course socialism. Government control. Confiscatory taxes. Look at Britain with that Socialist stooge Attlee as Prime Minister. 'A sheep in sheep's clothing' Churchill called him? Amusing, but wide of the mark, I'm afraid. He's busily abolishing British greatness. The Common Man," Father continued with an edge of contempt, "is having his day, and the Churchills and the Empire Builders and the Rugged Individualists are finished. High taxes alone can destroy individualism and enterprise and initiative and drive. We've had them during the war and that haberdasher Truman is going to continue them. He wants all of us to be like *him!*" he finished, with an incredulous raising of his bushy eyebrows.

"Taxes *were* pretty gruesome," said Wexford. "Didn't I read that nobody in this country could keep more than twenty-five thousand dollars a year after taxes?"

His father chortled involuntarily, wiped his mouth with his napkin, and then murmured, "That was their . . . attempt, I believe, yes."

Got around it, did you, Pop? Wexford reflected admiringly. Good old Pop.

After dinner, once more in the calm serenity of the library, sitting beside a crackling fire, highball in hand, Father said to Wexford, "You're going to turn eighteen in—"

"January."

"Yes. Well, it's time you knew about some financial arrangements I've been making for you, and for all you children. The year you were born I transferred three thousand dollars into a bank account in your name. I have done so every year since. That means you will be worth fifty-four thousand dollars on your birthday. Plus the appreciation this money has accumulated over the years."

Wexford's lively face became even more alive.

"Well! That *is* something. Gosh, I'm pleased. Fifty-four thousand dollars, plus."

"You are not to spend it, you are not to touch it. I will continue to give you three thousand dollars every year for as long as I live."

Wexford glowed with appreciation. "Why did you happen to hit on that particular sum, Father?"

"Under the tax regulations, even Roosevelt's destructive ones, I am allowed to give any member of my family that amount tax-free. So, when I die, all you children will already have a considerable amount."

And inheritance taxes dodged, reflected Wexford appreciatively. The rich do get richer, they surely do.

And hadn't Father's enterprise and foresight and intelligence and plain hard work made this fortune in iron ore and coal and natural gas? Didn't he have a right to protect it and hand it on?

"I don't know really what to say," rambled Wexford uncharacteristically. "You know what it does? It gives me—it makes me feel, I don't know, kind of free or something."

Father pulled slowly on his cigar. Its tip glowed contentedly. "That was," he finally murmured, "the idea. I've protected that money for you and the other children, now I want you, all of you, to protect it for the next generation. Freedom. Be yourself, do what you like, tell anybody who's against you that they can go screw themselves. That's what I wanted for you. And that's what I want to hand on."

There was a contemplative silence in the snug, firelighted room. The shining leatherbound sets of literary classics, the antique tables, ornamental bronze candlesticks, the quiet tacit glow of security and wealth, the leisurely sense of permanence, all struck Wexford once again. He had always felt an air of serene permanence in this house and this room in it.

Why then had he himself never enjoyed an inner
leisureliness and sense of security and permanence?
He was a driven person and he knew it. But *why*
was he?

He had just learned that his father had been building, and would continue to build, a private fortune
for him. He was doing well enough scholastically at
Devon, and could have been doing much better if
he'd taken the time, and he would do perfectly
acceptably at Harvard. Eventually he would go into
politics and go very far indeed, or else be a leading
political journalist, and he would do well at that too.
Just as he was probably the most notable member of
this class at Devon, and perhaps in the whole student body—notable in the literal sense of the word:
someone who was always noted, noticed—so he
would be in the great world beyond it later.

I'm going to be famous, Wexford decided, sitting
by the fire opposite Father. There's no doubt about
it.

For some reason, the family characteristics were
not his characteristics, his strengths, not at all. They
were serene and leisurely and secure. He was driv-
en. His own private sense of insecurity and urgency
would make him famous, influential. He *had* to be
superior, show it, prove it, shove it down other
people's throats. He could not brook people who
acted as though they were his equals. He did not
have friends, he had followers.

I'm a changeling, he thought there in the serene
library in his father's fine house. I don't know how I
came to be born into this family.

5

In Pete Hallam's American History class, relations among the students were not becoming any easier. He could cut off Hochschwender's references to the "Micks" and "mackerel snappers" when alluding to Irish immigration during the nineteenth century; he could tell Wexford that "Huns" and "Krauts" weren't appropriate designations for Germans. But he could not stem the swelling animus between these two bright, articulate, and somehow precociously bitter students.

They hated each other. But also and simultaneously they seemed to hate something about themselves. There was a curious, fundamental similarity between them which made their mutual aversion almost incendiary.

For a while Pete secretly found this enmity rather entertaining; he thought it made meetings of the class more stimulating; the atmosphere sometimes fairly crackled with animosity and masked insults.

But a little further into the fall term he began to sense an intensity coming into their exchanges which sounded almost hysterical around the edges, something unhealthy and possibly uncontrollable.

He was going to have to do something about it. He talked to both students' faculty advisers, but nei-

ther was able to provide him with any real help.
Their assessments of Hochschwender and Wexford
were oddly similar. "A special boy" . . . "undoubtedly bright, even gifted" . . . "seems to be basically
self-sufficient" . . . "not without a loyal friend or
two" . . . "probably will go places in whatever field
he eventually settles into." There were of course
divergences: Hochschwender was "a stickler for ful-
filling all his obligations," whereas Wexford was
"inclined to be lackadaisical, casual, trying to gloss
over duties with charm."

But they had become mortal enemies, and with no
other Master in the school in a position to witness or
even really be aware of this collision course, Pete
decided he himself had better intervene and defuse
the situation if he could.

On the Sunday night of his return from the weekend at Cape Cod with his family, Wexford found a
note summoning him to Pete's quarters in Pembroke
House, and when he entered Pete's spare, rather
dimly lit room he found Pete and also Hochschwender
sitting there.

He was given a glass of ginger ale and told to sit
down.

"I guess you guys know why I've asked you here,"
Pete began without preliminaries. "You've been
going at each other in class like a couple of Kami-
kaze pilots. Rivalry's one thing. Differences of opinion are one thing. But you two have let what looks
like a mutual gut-hatred develop and it's unhealthy
and to me unreasonable and I think we should talk it
out and get rid of it. It can only do you both harm. I
mean you'll do harm to yourselves, not each other."
Not each other I hope, he added warily to himself.

"Well," they both simultaneously drawled, and
then with disgusted looks lapsed into silence.

"Hochschwender?" said Pete.

"Well, sir, to me it doesn't seem unreasonable to point out what a fraud somebody is, faking information, covering up failure even to do his homework by a lot of what I think the Mi— the Irish call 'blarney.' "

Touché: Wexford indeed was frequently ill prepared and given to persiflage to conceal it.

Pete said, "Dealing with any student's lack of preparation is my business, not yours."

Hochschwender's lean, prowlike face looked disdainful.

Wexford eased in languidly: "Is it really unreasonable, sir, to undercut nakedly Fascist viewpoints in class? I mean, we've just fought a bloody war and—"

"I know about the bloody war," Pete cut in dryly. "And I know about the bankruptcy of Fascist ideas. All the students are here to further their education, the Masters are here too for that, in a way. But when Hochschwender comes up with views that are obnoxious to just about everybody, the job of education is to modify them, change 'em. But it's not part of it to do this by hurling insults, letting yourself get obviously—uh—choked with emotions, almost drowning in emotionalism. *That's* unreasonable."

"This is supposed to be a free country," said Hochschwender cuttingly. "There's supposed to be free speech here. This is supposed to be a 'liberal' school"—Hochschwender was master of putting quotation marks around any word he chose—"I'm just asserting one of the things you people fought that war for."

"Sir," exclaimed Wexford in a shocked tone Pete saw to be exaggerated, fake. "Isn't he a traitor? Do we have to stand for a Nazi baiting us in American History class!"

"Just reminding you of your principles, Mr. *Waxwork*, that's all."

Into Wexford's face rushed the reddish purple flush which had worried Pete in class. "You really are a Fascist pig," he said to Hochschwender in a very uncharacteristic, guttural voice.

Pete blew out an exasperated breath. Total failure. He couldn't bring off any truce or even barest mutual tolerance. Hopeless.

Pushing his hands on the tops of his knees he stood up. "That's all, boys. I want you to be civil to each other in my class and any fistfights or any of that outside of it will get you on Probation, or worse. That clear?"

The two proud, bright youths eyed him speculatively and conceded faint, unwilling nods. Again Pete saw the fundamental similarity which they also sensed and found unforgivable: it was unbearable to be forced to see an unmistakable parody of yourself in this other creep. That was the source of the hatred, and it would never run dry as long as Wexford remained Wexford and Hochschwender, Hochschwender.

* * *

On Monday Wexford went to his little glass-enclosed cubicle at *The Devonian* office. Through the window he could see a corner of the chill, snow-covered campus. And to think he was supposed at this moment to be on cross-country skis slogging through freezing woods. He shuddered inwardly. As long as there were winters like this one, and people had to live through them, New England Puritanism would never die.

On his desk were four letters to the editor. The first he opened demanded to know how soon maid service, an amenity of prewar Devon, would be restored. Wexford scrawled, "As soon as the Republicans get back into the White House" across it as an indication of the line he would take in answering it in print. The second letter recommended that Mrs. Pancoast, the school dietitian, be forced to eat her own food three hundred and sixty-five days a year and that the students take out a life-insurance policy on her, with themselves as beneficiaries. Wexford scrawled, "Too cheeky to print?" on this one, and went on to the third. It suggested that a course be established in the History Department on the origins of the First and Second World Wars. The letter was written by Evan Rodell, the presumptive valedictorian of the senior class, and was a very thoughtful and detailed outline of how such a course might be structured and what its benefits would be. "Page One," Wexford wrote across the top. He would print it in a special box and see whether this idea took hold. Rodell was bright. Wexford showered charm upon him every time they met, which was as infrequently as Wexford could manage. In a way he would have liked to bury this letter on a back page or ignore it altogether, but Rodell was too important for that, and besides, the idea was a good one and Wexford was in favor of good ideas. After all, not every good idea could come from himself.

The fourth letter, he was mildly surprised to see, was from Eric Hochschwender. It came brusquely to the point:

To the Editor:

Now that the war has ended in victory for our glorious democracy, it is time to jettison all excess baggage and relics of the past.

Compulsory daily Chapel at this school is a ridiculous opiate left over from another era. No serious person believes in that nonsense.

It must be abolished.

Let the students vote on it. We fought the war

for democracy, right? I say let's practice it, right here. Let's vote to get this phony mumbo-jumbo out of here.

> Yours,
> Eric Hochschwender

The letter was redolent of Hochschwender's truly remarkable Teutonic gall, or, as he must call it to Hochschwender's face sometime, *chutzpah*.

Hochschwender, mused Wexford, had all the charm of a Panzer attack. The crew-cut blond hair, the bony face, ice-blue eyes, too-rigid posture: he was like a parody of a Prussian. His reason for living seemed to be solely to irritate others.

And now he proposed to abolish Chapel, cancel God.

Not even the most flaming atheist could really have found anything offensive in these services at Devon. God had been shifted gently over the decades and through the centuries increasingly into the background at the school, so that now He was little more than a very distant, remote, patriarchal beneficence, dimly sensed perhaps somewhere up among the bells, a sort of abstract force for good, like nutrition.

The school had been founded by Puritans in the eighteenth century, true, but as the crises of conscience seized the divines and the academics all through the nineteenth century and Belief emerged battered and compromised almost out of existence in the twentieth, so God had been wafted into ever more remote recesses of the school.

There were still the hymns—"God of Our Fathers," "A Mighty Fortress," all the ones that young male voices sounded impressive singing; there were Responsive Readings, Gospel excerpts, a prayer or two, and that took care of God.

Now Hochschwender demanded the abolition of this subdued, tasteful, nondenominational, perfunctory morning service in which the real purpose, in any case, was not to worship God but to get all the students in one place each day so that announcements dealing, for example, with influenza warnings could be issued. Abolish Chapel! It was as empty and at the same time as inflammatory a proposal as an attack on Motherhood or the Flag.

Wexford understood rabble-rousing and acting as an *agent provocateur* instinctively and deeply, since both tendencies were in his bones. It took one to tell one, and fire must be fought with fire, and it took a thief to catch a thief, and Wexford found himself instantly primed to meet this challenge head-on.

Here, playing directly into his hands, was just the enemy he had been randomly probing for at Devon, out to destroy Our Traditions and Our Way of Life.

The letter was prominently printed in the next issue of *The Devonian*, alongside an editorial by Wexford denouncing it as "godless" and "corrupting" and "the thin edge of the wedge" and "a vicious attempt to undermine the foundations of the school" and "blasphemously un-American." (Even Rodell's letter about the new History course was after all buried on a back page. Controversy was news, Wexford's journalistic instincts told him.)

Hochschwender's letter by itself might have caused a flurry and been forgotten. But combined with the inciting editorial and others following it up, and a brace of offensive, arrogant letters from Hochschwender, the flame was whipped into a conflagration, faculty and alumni began to be sucked in, and the school seemed suddenly to be stumbling toward a major conflict.

"Look at that," said Hochschwender to Rob Willis in their room, "he fell for it. I knew he would."

"I don't quite see the point of it. Do you really want to abolish Chapel?"

"Of course not. Who cares? But. They hate everything German? *We're* barbarians? I wanted to smoke Wexford, and I've done it. *Now* you'll see intolerance, American style."

In Pembroke House The Boys lounged in chairs in the Butt Room and kicked the issue around. As varsity athletes they were not supposed to smoke. Some did and some didn't.

"Chapel is Chapel and religion is religion and God is God," someone observed.

"That's a big help."

"Well—"

"I think this guy Hochschwender doesn't like it here. Why doesn't he leave? Hell, Chapel is like, I don't know, the school band or something. It's just there. It's like the Academy Building. It isn't as though it really meant anything."

"It does to me. I believe in God."

"Well, my God, you don't need Chapel for that!"

"Why doesn't he just get out of here?"

"Maybe we ought to, you know, encourage him to leave, help him make up his mind."

"That's just what that Wexford guy wants us to do," said Tug Blackburn. "He's trying to stir up trouble." But his view was drowned out in a general reaction of hostility toward Hochschwender.

The next day Hochschwender returned to his room and found his bicycle in bits and pieces festooned all around it.

"Well, look what the tolerant American democrats have done!" he observed with satisfaction to Rob. "I wonder what they'll do next."

He was saved any further problem, however, by the arrival of Christ's birthday.

•　•　•

Pete Hallam stayed in his apartment in Pembroke House for the holidays. He had nowhere else to go. Just two years ago, in December 1943, in Italy, he had received a truly classic Dear John letter from his twenty-one-year-old wife:

My dear Peter,
This is the hardest letter I've ever had to write. I know how you value honesty and I have tried to too. I have met a man named George . . .

Secretly he had always suspected, feared, that his fate was to be ultimately alone—popular, admired, "well liked," and alone.

Within a day or two of the students' departure he found to his surprise that Devon opened itself to him to reveal a new dimension: there was a special charm to this little New England town without hordes of teen-age boys in it. The imposing array of school buildings unveiled their quiet dignity, the view of the campus swept unobstructed to river, forest and horizon. The raucous back wing of Pembroke House fell silent, the silence of a battlefield, he thought with a kind of rueful amusement, when the shooting has stopped and even the corpses have been carted away.

The school library, remaining open, acquired a restful, philosophical, brooding calm he would never have suspected. The river, with the famous sweep of black ice curving through the stripped, snow-filled woods, had about it a Robert Frost–like poetry, poised and hardy and elemental, now that the clatter of hockey sticks and the shrill shouts of players and the thud of body checks had been stilled.

One day he skated up the river alone: the doctors had advised continued exercise of his injured leg.

Peculiar place as I see it now, the Devon School, he was thinking.

All these boys, these not-yet-adults, perching here for a few years, thinking they know who they are, thinking they are in a position to judge one another, trying to present set, confident versions of themselves to the world and, all the while, babes in the woods really, self-ignorant and confused, at best very partial semi-adults, saying in effect: I'm completely sound and normal and a total human being and aware of everything about myself, while in reality they were most of them cross-eyed with confusion about themselves, insecure as a house on stilts in a hurricane, pretending manfully, or almost manfully, that they were not stumbling blindfolded into the pitfalls of their futures.

And now this witch-hunt or red herring or whatever it was about Chapel! What was this incredible Charlie Chaplin–Nazi Hochschwender up to? In Pete's American History class he exhibited to the hilt his arrogance, his amazing capacity for and apparent pleasure in offending everyone in sight. "Well of course the Civil War was just the North wanting to take over the South's markets. They didn't give a damn about the niggers!" "Everybody knows that America was colonized by tramps and criminals, the scum of Europe." At least two members of the class had ancestors who had come over on the *Mayflower*. "The Nazis learned genocide from America, of course, what you did with your Indians." It was characteristic of him to refer to Americans as "you." Hochschwender's family had been in Wisconsin for several generations.

After the remark about the "niggers" Pete had said, "Hochschwender, don't use that word here. Educated people don't. It"—unable to stop himself—"is as though I called you a Hun or a Kraut."

Hochschwender had smiled crookedly, somehow pleased.

And then there was Wexford. As part of his duties on the staff of the Department of Physical Education Pete was responsible for checking the attendance of students. Over the months a pattern of attendance or nonattendance began to emerge with regard to certain students. Pete developed a sort of sixth sense about it, just from looking over check-in lists. One of the names which gradually came into focus as dubious was Wexford's. The signatures were so strangely varied. And as he watched Wexford himself he thought that for someone officially in the open air for a couple of hours daily in the fall in New Hampshire, he was remarkably pale.

Pete's first impulse was to go and see Wexford in his dormitory about this. And then he caught himself. *I* am going to go and see *him*? What kind of a reversal was *that*? Somehow Wexford had been able to impose himself on the consciousness of the school in such a way as to make it for a moment seem natural for Pete to call upon him about this.

He sent for Wexford.

"I'll bet you like living in Pembroke House," began Wexford easily, smiling affably and sinking into an easy chair, longish legs stretched comfortably out before him. "Right at home with the athletes, eh?"

"We have some good players here," observed Pete.

"And some good ringers, too. I wonder"—his hazel eyes rolled cogitatively to the ceiling—"if we ought to do an editorial about that for the paper? 'Subsidized Athletes Dim Devon's Luster.' Something like that." He cocked his head with a look of smiling inquiry at Pete.

Pete contemplated him for a moment and then said, "I thought *The Devonian* was supposed to be a newspaper."

"It certainly is."

"Then why don't you stick to the news? Everybody knows we've had six football scholarships here for the last thirty years."

"Still," observed Wexford, leaning his head languidly against the back of the easy chair, "it might stir up quite a few people if we point it out again. This is *postwar* now, you know. Everything's got to be reexamined."

I think this schoolboy is trying to blackmail me, Pete said to himself sharply. You're quite a handful, aren't you, Master Wexford. I wonder where you're headed.

"Getting down to specifics, Wexford," he said briskly, "your attendance at golf looks peculiar to us." Two could use the editorial, royal, first-person plural. "Different-looking signatures. Coach Simpson says he's hardly ever seen you out there. What about it?"

Wexford rolled his eyes, head still cradled by the back of the chair, in Pete's direction. "I don't know what you mean, sir."

Never had "sir" sounded so subtly condescending before. "My handwriting . . . you see, my mother, I'm naturally left-handed, but my mother, a conformist lady if there ever was one, beside her Queen Victoria was a radical! My mother insisted that both my brother and I, both natural left-handers, be taught to write with the right hand. So my handwriting never got, so to speak, *placed*. It varies wildly." He paused. "Sorry." A fixed smile accompanied this, conveying, Are you going to fall for this ridiculous story? But on the other hand, what else *can* you do?

"What's wrong with your color?" cut in Pete, frowning. "You been to the Infirmary lately? Maybe you've got a low-grade infection. Better go over there for a physical."

"I assure you I don't—"

"Go over there for a checkup, and if the doctor checks you out as okay, we'll expect to see you daily out at sports, either one of the teams or at our regular Gym class, at two-thirty." He stood up.

Wexford rose rather languidly and said, "I feel perfectly fine."

"I'm a little worried about your pallor," said Pete.

"Well," Wexford laughed pleasantly, "it's nice to have the school *worried* about me."

"You know, Wexford," said Pete, patting him in a friendly and at the same time patronizing way on the back, "we do worry about the students while they are here, but what we're concerned about around here all the time is the good of the school."

"Of course," murmured Wexford, flashing a smile one last time.

As he slowly skated upriver on the black ice Pete was in fact concerned about the school. There was this unpleasant, subtle conflict slipping into it, seeping like escaping gas along the corridors, insinuating itself into Butt Rooms and classrooms, drifting over faculty dinners. It had been threatening to get serious, just before the vacation intervened.

This messy, unwieldy conflict concerned conformity, how much dissent could be contained here. Was dissent going to be persecuted? Could that be allowed? Could it be stopped? Could an obnoxious, phony, Hitlerian poseur be allowed to disrupt the school? Could he be expelled, simply for being obnoxious? Could he be hounded out by the others? Was that to be permitted? Could it be stopped?

On the other hand, in this solitude of his, Pete was probably letting this little schoolboy tempest grow all out of proportion in his imagination. After the Christmas break the boys would probably all come back full of hockey and nothing else. They usually did.

But in the back of his mind there lingered a continuing uneasiness. Hochschwender was such an implacable disrupter, a kind of tyrant or martyr, accepting no destiny in between.

And Wexford was a limitlessly ambitious conniver, momentarily trapped in adolescence.

Nothing could be more vicious than a fight between boys, lacking any trace of the caginess or caution of men.

6

Chapel the first day of the winter term proceeded normally. Hochschwender, Nick Blackburn noticed, was in his place. Since the senior class was seated alphabetically at the front of the Chapel, Nick could glance back and see Rob Willis signaling something to Eric Hochschwender. Hochschwender had a sardonic look on his face, as though he were being forced to participate in some child's game of bobbing for apples.

The service went on as usual. After a prayer and a hymn and some announcements the Headmaster read a rather lengthy passage from Stephen Vincent Benét's "The Devil and Daniel Webster" in his engaging, mellifluous voice, the passage about the Devil naming a jury for Jabez Stone's trial, summoning twelve great criminals from hell to be the jury of his peers.

Then the "service," if that was what it was, the school assembly really, ended and the students trooped out into a spectacularly cold New England morning. To the Blackburn boys, brought up in a border state, New England winters were literally breathtaking. On mornings such as this one the wind tearing by was so exceedingly cold that it did not seem possible to breathe it; it felt as though they were inhaling razor blades. Heads bent against the blast, Nick headed for his Latin class, Tug for Physics.

The first issue of *The Devonian* of the new term carried a special page-one boxed editorial, Wexford's most strident yet, entitled "Enemies of Our Victory." In it Hochschwender, not named, was accused of being part of a conspiracy to destroy America from within, since the Nazi-Fascist Axis had failed to destroy it from without.

Once again The Boys lounged around the Butt Room and discussed it. Nick happened to be there, seeing Tug.

"Well, Wexie Baby really let the Kraut have it."

"Couldn't we bury Hochschwender in a bunker somewhere and forget about him?"

"I wonder if Berchtesgaden is for rent?"

"We bombed that to smithereens."

"Wexford's just trying to cause trouble," said Tug stubbornly. "I told you before and I'll tell you again."

"Why don't we take apart *Wexford's* bicycle!"

A little tremor of pleasure passed through the room. Originality had reared its provocative head.

"I know. Let's write a letter to Wexford, supporting Hochschwender!"

"Is it too late to elect Hochschwender president of the class?"

"I want him for my roommate."

"You think he's free for spring vacation? My sister needs a boyfriend."

" 'Hochschwender Fair, O brother stern yet tender . . .' " someone began singing, a variation of the school anthem.

" '. . . Born with our land, and loyal now as then . . .' "

More voices were joining in.

" '. . . LONG HAVE YOU STOOD, UNCHANGED, OUR YOUTH'S DEFENDER . . . BIDDING US HITHER THAT WE MAY . . . BE . . . MEN!' "

What the *hell* is going on in there? Pete Hallam asked himself, hearing reverberations in his apartment. He made his way through the various narrow corridors to the back of the house. Poking his head in the Butt Room he said, "What's going on in here?"

"We're just serenading Hochschwender," replied Cotty Donaldson. "We've decided to elect him president of the class, if it isn't too late."

"Nooo, it isn't too late," said Pete with a small grin. He ambled comfortably back to his apartment. The Boys were turning the whole potentially explosive issue into a joke. Thank God a boy had a sense of humor. Without that, schools such as Devon would blow apart.

Two days later Wexford went to his *Devonian* cubicle and found another letter to the editor. It was from Cotty Donaldson.

To the Editor:

    On behalf of the entire varsity football squad I propose that Eric Hochschwender, Class of 1946, be appointed to compose the Class Prayer, in Latin, so he can read it at the Commencement ceremonies in June. I am assuming that he will be alive and well and living in Devon, New Hampshire, and not in Argentina, come June.

    We know it isn't the custom to have a Class Prayer, but then neither is winning a World War an annual custom. We are the first Class to graduate since that victory, and we feel a special commemoration is in order. Who better to speak for us than Eric Hochschwender? He is bursting with school spirit, reeks of loyalty to Class, school, and country.

    Do we hear any seconds?

Cotty Donaldson

So they're trying to make a joke out of it, Wexford reflected, running his fingers through his hair. Well, we'll see about that.

However, considering its source, he had no choice but to run the letter.

Two days later a reply arrived.

To the Editor:

Please convey this message to the members of the varsity football team.

Drop dead.

Eric Hochschwender

Beaming, Wexford rushed that into print, and awaited developments. But days went by, weeks, and there was no riposte from The Boys. Hochschwender did not have to endure short-sheeting of his bed, let alone finding a dog stool put in it. Nobody took a punch at him. Nobody insulted him, at least publicly.

It was very cold. The students went into a form of hibernation for the winter months, to study, contract colds, ski when possible, play basketball and hockey. The Glee Club gave a concert and everybody attended. What else was there to do?

They were buried in the upper reaches of New England, in an isolated little old town. They had been sent here to study, advance their educations, prepare themselves for Harvard, or if not, then Yale, or as a last resort, Princeton. The school was expensive. Scholarship boys felt they were being given a rare opportunity. The teachers were competent. Scholastic achievement settled over the white towers, the snow-buried campus, the steam-heated houses and dormitories and classrooms of Devon.

Wexford was reduced to writing editorials about Nature.

Hochschwender began studying the organ.

Pete Hallam concluded that there was nothing to worry about at the Devon School. It had survived the Articles of Confederation, Citizen Genêt, the burning of the White House, the Know-Nothings, Fort Sumter, Custer's Last Stand, the sinking of the *Maine*, Henry Ford, poison gas, Carry Nation, the New Deal, Hitler, and it was going to go on surviving.

The students hibernated as though they were bears. Pete Hallam sensed a mood of suspended animation setting in. Rage and prejudice and plain orneriness fell asleep for the winter.

In his padded cell beneath the Chapel Wexford strummed "Rustles of Spring." Surely it was true, he felt, that boys, even The Boys, would be boys. He swept on through "Rustles of Spring." At Devon, in spring, the young men's fancies did not lightly turn to thoughts of love. But they definitely did have to turn to *something*. Wexford would hibernate along with them through these frozen winter months, playing the piano, writing editorials about Nature, studying some, avoiding outdoor and indeed any exercise as usual, and wait for the first tumultuous, galvanizing rustles of spring.

7

Wexford was in the Readers' Retreat Room, reading the volume of *Remembrance of Things Past* called *The Captive*.

This is the most boring work of prose fiction ever written, he mused; only a great genius could have sustained it. Four hundred pages about a man ruminating on his jealousy.

I'm going to kill myself if I don't find something to do. I've got to get out of here. This school and this town are driving me crazy.

His mother was in Palm Beach for the winter, but that did not present Wexford with any problems. He forged a letter from her asking the Dean's office for permission for him to visit her at the family home on Cape Cod once again—it was closed for the winter—and this was routinely approved.

Friday evening Wexford checked into the Copley Plaza Hotel in Boston. Someone from Devon might just possibly see him there, but life was—*should be*—full of risks. First he bought four bottles of Scotch. Wexford could make himself look twenty-five years old at will, in a bankerish gray pinstripe suit, fedora, and a suggestion of a sneer on his face. If all else failed, he had his fake identification cards.

Changing into slacks, sweater and a raincoat, he

went to the Old Howard burlesque house off Scollay Square, and then to two seedy bars nearby. He roamed into a taxi dance hall far down Washington Steet, and as he drifted around he fell into conversation with bums, drunks, whores, drifters, an AWOL soldier. He couldn't disguise an overtone of British, upper-class speech he had somehow acquired. It was a different accent from that of any other member of his family, anyone at school, in fact anyone anywhere in the world, but it was his and he would—could have no other. When some thug or whore asked him just what he was doing in this kind of bar, he would explain that he was a graduate student in sociology at Harvard doing research. Whether they believed this or not, they were quite sure that no one with such a highfalutin', affected way of talking could conceivably be a cop, and so they drank comfortably with him. He bought the drinks.

Wexford also fit in well because of something else about him, his wayward look. The wide-set eyes with their shifting shades, lock of reddish hair loose on his forehead, and above all the rather wide, too-expressive mouth, the mouth of a charmer and a liar, all these lulled them. So did his professionally beaming smile, his giggle and sneer, and a strange, decadent *O* his mouth sometimes briefly formed, the mouth for an instant of a toothless, old androgynous crone.

For his part, Wexford was not afraid to venture alone and a little drunk into this world. Although his clothes were chosen to be as nondescript and everyday-looking as possible, the way he readily picked up the checks betrayed his difference from them. He felt sure however that he would not be attacked in a dark alley, given a Mickey Finn, rolled. His sense of destiny assured him that these humiliations wouldn't happen to him. They just wouldn't. These people somehow wouldn't dare.

Rather late Saturday night, after going to a performance of the Boston Symphony, where his own
obbligato of Scotch before, during, and after the
performance contributed much, Wexford found himself in an excited little bar somewhere: a piano jan-
gled away out of sight in a corner, servicemen and
students and couples and single girls and older
women mingled and laughed and struggled through
the crowd up to the bar. The drinks were flowing,
shouts and squeals and guffaws crowded the smoky,
stuffy air. Wexford eventually succeeded in shoul-
dering his way up to the bar for another Scotch.

He was very pleasantly drunk. An invisible shield
enclosed him and made him safe and happy and
untouchable. He leaned against the bar in his very
dark gray flannel suit, maroon-and-gray-striped tie
and Brooks Brothers shirt, and prepared to give himself the special pleasure of sitting back silently to
contemplate the follies of those around him.

There were two young men in Air Force flight
jackets deep in conversation at the far end of the
bar. Wexford was positive that they were telling
each other war stories and equally positive they would
be telling those same stories to anyone who would
listen thirty years in the future. There was a couple
so intimately entwined in embraces, kisses, soulful
gazes, and sensual strokes that Wexford knew that
their relationship was a sexual failure. At least one,
possibly both, of them lacked any desire for the
other, hence the public exhibition. There was a live
wire of a little man in a porkpie hat scooting from
group to group, the resident clown apparently, who
never left any of them until he could leave them
laughing. He noticed a couple, she in a fur-trimmed
dark leather coat, he in a camel's hair coat. They
were perhaps in their late twenties. She was good-
looking and aware-looking, surveying the room with
large, very dark brown eyes. He was tall and rather

pale and in some way distinguished, and also seem-ingly semi-drunk. At one point she appeared to be looking at Wexford; so did he. Then they both went on surveying the room.

I wonder if they're even Americans, he mused idly. Their clothes look American, but there seemed to be something European about them—French, or maybe Italian, Italian aristocrats, from Rome. Her father has a Papal title, Wexford decided. He can trace his ancestry back to Caesar Augustus. They use cocaine.

His eyes roamed over other groups and solitary drinkers; then he procured another Scotch for him-self. Suddenly he saw the young woman in the dark brown leather coat making her way, it seemed, toward him, with her companion in tow. She stopped in front of him. "Whose looks do you like, mine or his?" she demanded with a mocking smile in a low-pitched, strictly American voice. "Quick. Don't stop to think. Him or me?"

"I, well, I guess I *was* staring, wasn't I? Sorry. I was just thinking—you do want to know what I was thinking, don't you?"

"I'll say."

"I was thinking that you two looked too, well, sophisticated or something for this particular bar."

"And we were thinking," she said with slightly widened eyes, "that you looked like a good lay."

Wexford, totally knocked off-balance, struggled to say, laughing confusedly, "I don't know anything about that!"

"You don't?" she demanded, eyes widening a lit-tle more. "Well, laddie, you've found the right peo-ple to show you. Look. It's late. Brian and I, this is my husband, Brian, by the way. I'm Jenny. Our apartment's not far from here." She studied his face with those large, all-seeing eyes. "You want to come over? Come on. We can talk about it all there . . . talk about it . . . or," a quick grin, "whatever else we want to do . . . all three of us . . . or you and me . . . or," she finished airily, "you and him. Want to?"

The invisible shield protecting Wexford lay in ruins. Stunned, he tried somehow to avoid her encompassing eyes. "I um," a forced laugh, "I'm just hanging around here . . . waiting for my date to show up." Nervously, he checked the eyes. They weren't going for this story."

"Dear one," she said smoothly, even sympathetically, "you don't have any date meeting you here. Scared? You scared of us?"

"No," he said truthfully, "of course not."

"Then why not? We're not going to bite you. Maybe I made the whole thing seem too sudden or strong or I don't know. Why don't we all just go over to our place for one nightcap and get to know each other better, and then it's good-night and maybe we'll get together another time soon."

The whole proposition abruptly became too much for Wexford. "Sorry," he said rather formally, "I've really got to go. Good-night . . . and," somehow felt called on to add, "thank you—for everything." He writhed inwardly on hearing these idiotic words.

As he edged away Wexford felt her searchlight eyes following him, analytically, not unsympathetically either, perhaps even, well, with pity. Terrible. Pity. He pushed his way brusquely through the last of the crowd and was out the door into the chill night air.

What did they *mean* by coming up to him like that! What did they take him for, some kind of male prostitute?

A woman full of sexual aggression and her fairy husband, two utter strangers, try to drag him back to their apartment for some kind, or all kinds, of sex. He was shaking, he was enraged to find; it was all an uncontrollable—something, an uncontrollable challenge. *He* was supposed to issue the challenges. She was a really devastatingly, literally devastatingly magnetic woman. The husband was a mysterious, intriguing, silent figure. They had thrown out the bluntest conceivable sexual challenge.

He had got to stop shaking. Who did they think he was!

Well, who was he, sexually?

He was not ready for them or it or any variation or combination of possibilities like that, not here and not yet and not now and maybe never; it was mortifying and sickeningly exciting and an abasement and it shook his hold on himself. Was it shaky, that hold? Wexford began to walk very briskly toward a taxi idling at the corner, walking away from that bar. He meant to get it as quickly and completely as possible out of his thoughts and his memory and his consciousness and his experience and he knew that he could not.

He drank enough Scotch back in his room at the Copley and eventually got to sleep, awoke, headachy and stunned but still able to pull himself together for a late morning walk. Wexford came back to the hotel for lunch and then, wandering around, found himself in front of one of the friendly bars off Scollay Square he had visited Saturday afternoon. He decided to go in for a Scotch to complete his recuperation. Everything about Saturday night was to be put completely out of his mind, everything.

This bar had a pervasive, soaked-in, ineradicable aroma of stale beer. It was a long, narrow, rather dark room, light coming through the big pane of glass facing the street and from a few dim lights at the rear, where there were some pinball machines and a pool table.

A young man was playing one of the pinball machines. In a booth halfway toward the back an old-young woman with a teen-ager's hairdo and a lined, drawn face sipped a beer and confided in a man with the back of his head to Wexford.

Then a half-dozen young men came noisily through the entrance, wearing Army pants and pea coats and other remnants of service uniforms. They bellied up to the bar next to Wexford and ordered beers. All were wearing the "Ruptured Duck" discharge insignia. Here were the national heroes and celebrities of 1946, veterans.

They took gulps of their beer and began talking about housing and how hard it was to find and last night's bowling and Harvard's basketball loss the day before—"the Harvards never get anybody who can play *basketball*, hockey maybe, never basketball" —and the GI Bill of Rights, and one of them, losing interest in their conversation, a little high, turned to Wexford and asked forthrightly, "Who're you?"

"Oh—I—well—"

"Where's your duck? Don't you wear your discharge pin? You look like a 4-F without it."

"As a matter of fact—" *I'm still in school,* he was going to say but there was the bartender listening with interest and Wexford was breaking the law here.

"I guess I forgot it this morning."

"What outfit were you in?"

"The Air Force, Fifth Air Force. In England." Too late he remembered that his brother was in the *Eighth* Air Force in England.

"Fifth Air Force in England!" cut in a short, square-faced man. "If the Fifth Air Force was in England I'm Hirohito."

"The Eighth, of course, that's what I meant. I tell you, drinking Scotch this early in the day will—"

"What was your duty?"

"I was a navigator, I only came in at the very end and—"

"Is that right," said the first one with a grimace. "England was good duty by then. Where were you stationed?"

Wexford's swift mind was a featureless blank. London became the only city in England he could think of. Then the name "Coventry" in connection with airplanes popped into his mind and he said it.

"We had no air base at Coventry," the oldest-looking of the group joined in, a disgusted tone to his voice. "Look, I don't give a damn if you were 4-F or a sex pervert or what, but I do care when some punk goes around impersonating a veteran."

Wexford stared deep into his Scotch and then murmured, "I'm not impersonating anybody."

"Cal," he asked the bartender, "you know this guy?"

"Nope." Red-faced, with white curly hair, Cal the bartender leaned across in front of Wexford. "You got any I.D. on you?" he asked quietly.

Suddenly Wexford felt a cold grip of rage at the back of his head. "Why do I need identification? *I* know who I am. I had drinks here yesterday. You didn't need any identification *then*. Why is it different now that these—people are around? The hell with identification." Face flushed, he swallowed a mouthful of Scotch.

The oldest veteran's hand took a firm grip on the back of his right hand. "Identification," he said. Wexford turned to look into a pair of fixed blue eyes.

The cold seizure of rage clamped itself harder. Wexford snatched his hand away and blurted, "Keep your hands off me. Understand?" He felt the rage shaking up through him like a thrust of power, a great surge of strength, invincibility.

A hand slammed against the back of his neck and he was hauled to his feet. "Out!" a voice growled in his ear; another hand seized the seat of his pants and as he was hustled toward the door someone opened it and Wexford was hurtled out on the sidewalk, leaving a wave of laughter in his wake.

I'll kill them, he thought. I need a gun. I'll throw a—what do the Russians call those incendiary bombs? A Molotov cocktail. That's it. I'll burn out that bar.

And as he moved away and then began to tramp block after Boston block, not seeing what he was passing, walking with a rapid fury, the exercise began to clear and quicken his brain. I won't find a gun today: I won't be able to kill them. I can't make a Molotov cocktail, not today.

Someday, some year, sometime, I will be able to retaliate and win. There won't be any humiliation, no, nor any challenges either, no one someday will want to challenge me. Not me. I'd rather be dead than ground down by goons like that. I've got pride. I deserve to have it and I've got it: pride.

After picking up his bag he took a taxi to North Station, thinking, all things considered, that it hadn't been such a bad weekend, just some unfinished business left for the future. As chilly dusk crept over the upright, old-fashioned streets of Boston, semi-deserted on Sunday, he considered with some satisfaction that this truant weekend had really had a lot of variety, and that was the spice of life.

It had had a strikingly varied set of characters and scenes, backdrops and playhouses. He thought of it all in these theatrical terms: he saw life as theater and himself always and everywhere as of course the leading actor, playing roles comic and tragic and satirical, heroic and corrupt, funny and threatening, varied, rich and risky and ceaseless. This was living.

And then inevitably, glumly, it was 5:15 P.M. Sunday and he was on board the Boston-and-Maine coach clickety-clacking prosaically back to deep-in-the-country Devon. Why? He'd outgrown the place by now. Why did life have to *hold him back* so much?

Wexford tried to read *The Captive* on the train. It was unbearable; the emotion of jealousy was being analyzed by Proust literally to death, and those dying might include the reader. He *had* to do something else.

He started thinking of Hochschwender out of force of habit, and from that subject his thoughts drifted to the school Chapel—such harmless little rituals were conducted there; he questioned whether Lucifer himself would have objected—then idly he gazed back in his mind to the late war.

The opportunities Wexford would have had in it were limitless. If ever there was a *stage* it was World War II, if ever there was a drama, if ever there had been a backdrop for heroes—and look at the impressive lineup, obscure men thrust into national and even world fame—General Wainwright and the Bastards of Bataan; Commander Kelly diving his plane down the smokestack of a Japanese battleship; Ernie Pyle, the war correspondent to end all war correspondents; GI Joe, the quintessential Common Man gone to war; Jimmy Doolittle bombing Tokyo from *Shangri-la*; Edward R. Murrow and "This is London"; Douglas MacArthur and "I shall return"; the Marines raising the flag on Iwo Jima . . .

Well he had missed it and that was that and on the other hand he just might have been killed. His sense of destiny might make him feel immune to any threats on Scollay Square but it could not withstand the entire holocaust of World War II. It would have been very much like himself, he realized, to volunteer for some hideously dangerous mission, flying an experimental plane over France loaded with explosives, the way the oldest of the Kennedy boys, neighbors on Cape Cod, had done, and been blown like him into Kingdom Come.

There were compensations for having been only seventeen years old on V-E and V-J Days.

Chapel . . . World War II . . . that outlandish Hochschwender . . . men dying in the war . . . perishing . . . What about . . . why not . . . Of course. Of course!

There must be a memorial to them, the Devon dead, and it must be a window, a beautiful stained-glass window, behind the altar, a very beautiful stained-glass window installed with all due ceremony and solemnity in the Chapel as a permanent memorial to the Devon students who had been killed in the war.

It was a great idea and its possibilities were formidable and there would be no torpor for Wexford at Devon for the rest of his year there. He could feel the boredom of clickety-clacking back to Devon fall away from him, his mind began to make connection after stimulating connection, and a Purpose bloomed in his consciousness like a radiant spray of chrysanthemums.

• • •

"I want to talk to you," Wexford said brusquely to Tug Blackburn. They were walking down the steps of the First Academy Building after classes and out into the snow-piled campus. Proceeding across it in the direction of Pembroke House, Wexford swiftly outlined the plan for the Memorial Window.

"Sounds good to me," commented Tug briefly.

"You and Cotty Donaldson and your brother, if you three push this—and I will in the paper of course—then the whole school will go along and it'll be a great contribution from our class."

Tug cogitated. "I think you've got something there," he eventually conceded. The source of such a sterling idea, Wexford, had taken him aback for a moment, but now he had to admit its worth. And abruptly he conceived a much higher opinion of Wexford.

In the Butt Room a handful of The Boys who happened to be there considered it.

"I think it's a pretty good idea."

"It's uh I think, well, it's something we could do."

"It would be leaving a mark from our class. We won't have anybody on the Roll of Honor or whatever the hell they call it. You know. The guys who got bumped off."

"I think that's the point," put in Wexford. "I don't think the Class of 1946 should just sort of fade away anonymously. We ought to leave some kind of a *mark* around here. Let 'em know we were here once, the guys who'll be sitting in that Chapel fifty years from now staring up at that window." Wexford used the word "guys" only when dealing with The Boys, and then only when, as now, he wanted something from them. "Those guys will see we wanted them to remember the ones who . . . went to the war . . . and . . . didn't come back."

A grunt of approval could be heard. Wexford had found just the right phrasing, he noted with satisfaction. "Got killed" would have been too blunt; "sacrificed their lives" would have been much too corny. "Didn't come back" was just right: understated, plain, final.

He knew that this bunch of athletes had been leery of him until now. They had found something a little la-di-da about him, thought him too bookish, too sedentary.

Now he had made the one idealistic proposal they couldn't make fun of, "cut down," jeer at. They would have done so with virtually anything else. But not this. Pete Hallam might possibly take a jaundiced view of it, having been in action, wounded, taken prisoner, escaped. But not these unbloodied youths here. They felt too guilty, too subtly, subconsciously guilty. This was the one idealistic cause they would have to support to the hilt.

Wexford grinned at the room. They looked back at him with expressions of guarded, qualified, provisional approval.

8

Afterward Pete Hallam wondered why he had not obliterated this idea at the very outset. It had been so—well—if not transparent, then at least translucent, and the light shining through should have illuminated for him the implicit dangers.

No premonitions came to him at the time. He was sitting in his quarters in the evening, a few hours after Wexford's Butt Room meeting with The Boys. He answered a knock at the door and there stood Wexford, wearing a heavy knitted toboggan cap and a thick banditlike scarf across his lower face.

"This place certainly is cozy," he said, coming in.

And indeed with the fire burning in the fireplace and only a small table lamp and reading lamp adding more illumination, the dark wood paneling acquired a burnished warmth, and the heavy old furniture looked welcoming and comfortable.

Wexford struggled out of the toboggan cap, scarf, gloves, sheeplined duffel coat, galoshes. "Winter!" he snarled. "What bloody good does it do anybody? Why didn't they establish this school in Palm Beach?"

"When Devon was established Palm Beach was a Spanish bayou full of water moccasins and alligators."

"Well . . ."

"This climate's got vigor," Pete said with a shade of mockery. "That's what we want to get into you guys. What's that Dartmouth song? 'The granite of New Hampshire/In their muscles and their brains.' We want to get some granite into your brains."

Wexford chuckled a little nervously.

"How's the cross-country skiing?" asked Pete.

"Oh it's um stimulating. Like a nature walk."

"Where do you usually go?"

"Up the river, past the cannons."

"Not on the same side as the cannons? There's nothing but thick woods there."

"No, naturally, on the other side, past the Stadium. Beautiful country."

"Yeah. Ever get as far as Pierson's Knoll?"

One lightning glance from Wexford's greenish eyes shot at him and then came the easy answer, "I don't think so. Some of the other guys go that far. I'm just basically lazy, I guess."

There was no Pierson's Knoll. "Have a chair there by the fire," said Pete. "Like a Coke or something?"

"Coke," Wexford sighed. "In two days I will be old enough to die for my country. As a matter of fact I am now. Plenty of gu— fellows enlisted when they were seventeen and some of them got killed. And still here at Devon we must not be allowed *any* *liquor*. Christ." He seemed genuinely disgusted, and it struck Pete that in fact there was something precociously mature about Wexford, an experienced air which did make the offer of a Coca-Cola seem a little ludicrous.

"Well, I guess," Pete admitted, "rules applied equally to everyone are a little dumb. Some of the boys here won't be ready to drink at twenty-five, or really ever. Others—"

"How about a shot, Pete?" said Wexford swiftly, with a curving smile and an I-dare-you glint in his eye.

Pete drew a slow breath. He gazed at him from the other side of the fireplace and then said quietly, "Forget it."

There was a short silence and then Wexford said, "I've got a really good idea for a project for our class. Listen to this and tell me what you think." He outlined the plan for the memorial stained-glass window. Pete listened tranquilly and at the end shrugged and said, "Well, if your class wants to do that, raise the money, get a design the school will approve of, it might be okay. That window there now isn't much to look at. I think they must have run out of money when it came to the Chapel windows. Get some other students to come in with you and I'll set a meeting with the Headmaster and the Dean." He sat silent and then said, "It might turn out to be a contribution to the school, I guess."

His tone showed his doubts. Wexford sponsoring a religious window to the war dead? There was something wrong somewhere. Or was he just being suspicious and cynical, a battered, dried up "veteran," as everybody insisted on calling all servicemen who had ever heard a shot fired in anger. Wasn't he just a burned-out survivor who thought memorials were for the birds, heroism close to nonexistent, and wars meant to be forgotten as quickly as humanly possible?

Had one of the Blackburn boys, for instance, all bright-eyed and sincere, come to him with the idea, he would have endorsed it with a show of enthusiasm. He would have been touched, as a matter of fact, by the naïve idealism of it. What put him off was this slippery customer here having suggested it.

I'm too suspicious, he thought. This boy's after all not yet eighteen years old and he wants to make some kind of a contribution here.

"I'm for it," Pete finally said.

• • • •

The following Saturday the frigid weather which had clamped itself on Upper New England like a Nordic curse at last lifted, and the morning broke out a rich and blue canopy of spacious sky over this low-lying country. The sun reigned on a glittering campus of immaculate, silvery snow, and in Pembroke House some of The Boys felt they had to erupt or expire.

Tug and his roommate Cotty Donaldson and three others, Guy and Chet and R.T., stopped to pick up Nick Blackburn at his dormitory and then headed instinctively toward the Playing Fields. They tramped past the gray mass of the Gym and the capacious red-brick Cage, across the wide white expanse of the Playing Fields to the arching stone footbridge which spanned the Devon River here.

As they came up to it Cotty Donaldson playfully shouldered Tug Blackburn aside, forcing him to bump into the stone side of the bridge.

"Don't do that," said Tug.

"Not wide enough for all six of us to walk abreast," said Cotty airily.

"Well then—" said Tug, pushing him forcefully away.

"That wasn't really friendly," said Cotty, taking a handful of the front of Tug's thick sweater.

Tug instantly knocked the hand away. "Keep your goddam hands off me."

"You're getting carried away," said Cotty, shoving him against the side of the bridge.

Putting the heel of his hand against his chin, Tug forced Cotty back.

The sides of Cotty's hands chopped down on Tug's shoulders. "*Don't* start punching me around, you jerk."

Tug threw a punch at him, partially blocked, and then these two athletes were suddenly throwing fast punch after punch at each other. Like an accident, it happened with unreal suddenness.

"We've got to stop 'em before—"

"This is crazy. Don't—"

Cotty hit Tug a heavy right to the eye.

"Cut this *out*! Are you—"

"We—"

"This is—"

"Cut it out! For Christ's—"

Cotty was behind Tug and had a hammerlock around his throat.

"Oh, the hell with it. Let 'em go."

"What if somebody breaks something? The coaches'll be—"

"We can't just let two guys—"

Tug bent over and hurled Cotty over his head, then pounced on him on the ground.

"Can you grab Tug's legs?"

"If I jump Cotty—"

"What'll Pete say? Black eyes!"

"O *Je*-sus. I can't watch. Euh. Listen, we better *stop* this. They're really—somebody's gonna—"

By now the two fighters were off the bridge, rolling in the snow punching each other, and downed as they were, Nick Blackburn and the others were able to pull them apart.

Nick and R.T. sat on Tug, and Guy and Chet sat on Cotty, pinning them to the snow.

"Is that it?" asked Nick. "Is Jack Dempsey through for the day?"

"What about Gene Tunney over there?" panted Tug. "Ask him."

"Is that it over there?" asked Nick.

"You through?" said Guy to Cotty.

"I think one of my teeth is loose," mumbled Cotty, who was bleeding from the nose.

"That's why my knuckle's bleeding," mumbled Tug.

"We're going to get off you if you say you're through," said Nick.

"Yeah I guess . . ."

"Can we let you up?" Guy asked Cotty.

"Uh-huh."

They all got to their feet. Cotty leaned his head far back to stop his nosebleed. There was a swelling developing on Tug's right brow. They eyed each other over the shoulders of their friends.

"I still would like to break his face," muttered Tug in an undertone to Nick.

"Come on," said Guy to Cotty. "I want you two guys to—"

"None of that shaking hands crap," said Cotty.

"But look, you're roommates."

"That can be fixed."

"How? In January?"

Nick said, "Let's all go over to the Stadium and run a few laps."

"The Stadium track's got a foot of snow on it."

"So much the better. Makes it harder. Better for the leg muscles. Here we go!" and he trotted over the footbridge and on toward the two concrete banks of seats flanking the snow-covered football field a short distance away.

The other five students could think of no alternative to this, and so they began to trail after him.

It was one of the glowing days of deep winter which come now and then to New Hampshire. A grove of spruces at one end of the Stadium, a stand of towering pine some distance away, the frozen river nearby, the still, muffled atmosphere of snow-buried land combined to render these Fields Beyond, as they were called, remote and serene from the trust and clamor of the school.

The pure air pumping in and out of their lungs and the ease coming into their muscles as they labored in a plodding trot through the snow around the

Stadium track began to let the tensions flow out of them.

After they had circled the track several times, Cotty, winded, muttered out of the side of his mouth as he pulled alongside Tug, "You really are a jerk," in a reconciling tone of voice.

"Yeah, I know. I learned it from you."

"Where'd you learn to punch like that?"

"I've got a brother to practice on."

"*That's* what I've been lacking." They trotted on side by side for a minute and then Cotty added, "Will you be like my little brother? So I can learn to punch too?"

"You just had your first try. Enjoy it?"

"Noooo!" groaned Cotty.

The early northern dusk began to fall, with blue shadows creeping into the woods and across the snow, and a warning Arctic chill riding in on the evening wind. They headed back toward the formidable shapes and the graceful cupolas of the school.

They straggled up to the battered door in the back wing of Pembroke House, and there Tug came face to face with Pete Hallam, coming out.

"What the hell happened to *you!*" demanded Pete.

"Who uh me?" mumbled Tug.

"Yes. You."

"I . . . fell."

"No, you didn't fall. Are you guys going to start lying to me? You've been in a fight."

"Well . . ."

"Yeah," put in Cotty, "Tug and I, well we kind of lost our tempers and one thing led to another."

"What was the fight about?" asked Pete, squinting irritably.

"Well . . ."

"Let's see . . ."

"It was, well," Cotty said, "about how we were

going to go over the bridge at the river, how many abreast. You know.''

Pete contemplated them. "You had a fight about *that*?" He then said sourly, "That's what you were fighting about?"

They smiled sheepishly. The puerility of it all hit them as they looked at this man who had been wounded in battle.

"Go on," he said roughly, "get cleaned up. You're going to look like the joke of the week in the dining hall."

He shouldered his way through them, heading for dinner. But he couldn't shake off a sense of the oddness of it: Cotty Donaldson and Tug Blackburn, closest friends, fighting over who would cross a bridge first. It seemed that violence in people was ceaseless and eternal and everywhere.

Yes, but—the recollection forced itself upon him— hadn't he himself punched and bruised his wife one night, before going overseas, after a number of drinks, because she had . . . what had been his reason? She had laughed at him, mocked him a little, for saying that being a soldier was the final test of manhood or some such bullshit.

And he had loved her then . . .

• • •

The following day, Sunday, was equally beautiful and called forth another burst of outdoor energy. That evening the dining room at the Devon Inn was full. Sunday dinner at the Inn: it was a tradition.

Choosing to celebrate his birthday on Sunday, Wexford invited his group to dine there with him.

Tug and Nick Blackburn's father had arrived that morning for a quick visit, and he invited them there for dinner.

Pete Hallam's divorced wife had driven up from Boston to see him, and Pete invited her there for dinner.

The Inn, though built as late as the 1930s, had successfully been given an eighteenth-century patina, red-brick, unadorned Georgian.

The dining room, with its wainscoting and floral wallpaper, recessed windows, white linen tablecloths, its high ceiling and air of genteel comfort, provided the kind of country-hotel cooking—lamb chops, New England boiled dinner, scrod—deprived traveling salesmen working Upper New England would drive miles out of their way for. It was also several cuts above that served in the Devon School dining halls.

Wexford and his four followers sat at a circular table under a brass chandelier near the center of the room.

Wexford was unfailingly polite and ostentatiously friendly and considerate to the semi-outcasts who made up his group. He kept them steadily amused. He gave them weighty advice. He invited them to his family's house on Cape Cod for weekends. They were devoted to him.

For his part, very privately he thought of them as A, B, C, and D. He knew that sooner or later, certainly by the time he got to Harvard, they would be replaced by E, F, G, and H, who in turn would eventually give way to I, J . . . and so on. Life was change.

"Who is that glamour girl with our Mr. Hallam?" he asked C.

C craned his long thin neck, with thin hair growing far down it. "I think that's—didn't somebody say his wife was coming up to see him?"

"Ex-wife," murmured Wexford.

"Yeah. Somebody said at breakfast she was due up here. Alimony or something."

"I heard she wanted a reconciliation."

"Well, the story I got was . . ."

There were not a great many extracurricular hap-

penings to discuss at Devon, and any unusual move
made by some member of the faculty, especially one
as popular and admired as Pete, was instantly noticed,
speculated about, and beadily eyed observed.

"I should have taken you to Carson's," Pete muttered to Joan, naming the only other eating place,
barring diners, the town afforded. "Here it's like
eating in Macy's window."

"I don't mind," she said. "I like to get a taste,
anyway, of the atmosphere around here."

Students, most of them sitting with parents or
other older people, were surreptitiously eyeing her.
There were not many attractive young women to be
seen around Devon, and Joan Mitchell Hallam was
an attractive young woman. Her dark blonde hair
curved smoothly around her head, falling almost to
her shoulders, the ends curved inward, pageboy
style. A black band curved across the top of her
head and was tied under her hair; she wore large,
thin, gold circles of earrings, and a fashionable black
dress.

"It's all so *peaceful*," she sighed, leaning back, her
long neck extended, drawing a relaxed breath. "Soooo
peaceful." She helped herself to a popover. "You
must find it a lifesaver, after the—war in Italy, *prison
camp*, and well—"

"It's a good place," he said, "in a way."

"The boys must just adore you."

Pete speared some string beans.

"But is this—do you—see yourself here—more or
less permanently or . . ."

He took a cogitative breath. "Who knows? It's fine
for now."

"Just being," she laughed encouragingly, "here,
instead of in some prison camp—in the valley of the
Po! I'm sure that means a lot!"

She buttered her popover. "Pete"—she frowned

over her smile—"I don't know how to talk to you, reach you, anymore."

"No?" he said conversationally.

"You ought to help me."

He looked up at her with his light blue eyes. "Honey, I'm just not in the helping-people business anymore. I live from day to day up here. I do my job. Get along with these kids. That's all I've got. Nothing else to offer. Nothing else left maybe." He looked up at her again with his unforgiving northern blue eyes. "You're going to have to help yourself."

• • •

"That's Pete Hallam," said Nick to his father. "And that's his ex-wife." A disapproving frown settled on his lively face. "She wrote him a Dear John letter, in prison camp!"

"What is a Dear John letter?"

"It's a letter guys overseas got from their wives or sweethearts, kissing them off."

"Kissing them off?" repeated Mr. Blackburn. "I'm really beginning to feel completely out of touch."

"That means," said Nick patiently, "ditching them. Isn't that a pretty rotten thing to do? There your guy is, on the other side of the world, miserable, getting shot at, and you ditch him. By letter. But hers was the worst I ever heard about. Pete had been wounded, gotten captured and held in some pesthole of a prison camp in Italy. And she writes to him and says, 'Dear, I can't tell you how sorry I am. I love somebody else now. Bye.'"

Mr. Blackburn frowned in his turn. "Yes, that certainly is a deep betrayal." He looked at his two healthy sons, Tug husky, with his open, no-nonsense face, and Nick more finely drawn, eager, almost too alert. "Well," said Mr. Blackburn slowly, "you two boys just did escape by the skin of your teeth all kinds of hazards." He smiled at them.

Both frowned back. "Yeah but that's just it," began

Tug. "I feel kind of *funny* about that sometimes. Biggest happening of our lifetimes probably and we *missed* it, for God sakes."

"Yes it was for God's sake," said Mr. Blackburn quietly, "or by God's will."

"We sat up here in a private boys' school," put in Nick, "and all kinds of adventures were happening all over the world to millions of guys and not one thing happened to us."

"You were underage."

Tug said, "We could have enlisted the day we turned seventeen, which in my case was almost a year ago. We're just left out, that's all. Oh of course I didn't want to get killed or wounded or even shot at, but I did want to see something. I feel like I'm getting pretty old and nothing's happened to me. Sometimes I feel nothing ever will. I just play football. Big deal. They cheer at us. Bigger deal. Sometimes, you know what? Somebody gets hurt. Actually hurt. A sprained ankle maybe. Or, three years ago, a guy actually broke his leg. And that's about the size of it. Otherwise, we're just schoolboys. I feel like I've been a schoolboy forever, and I've got four more years of it, at least. Harvard," he finished in a distasteful tone.

Nick added, "We saw all those newsreels. All that artillery firing, all those naval guns, all those assaults on beaches in the Pacific, we saw those great film shots of the liberation of Paris, the people going wild and the soldiers riding down the boulevards in their Jeeps and tanks with flowers thrown at them, drinking wine. One of the great moments. And not just that. Special training. Paratroops. Frogmen. Spies. We missed it. Nothing's going to ever happen to us. There hasn't been anything in the air to breathe since I was fourteen years old but the war. And now the damn thing is over and all I ever was in were Civil Defense drills."

Mr. Blackburn looked at them silently for a few moments. Finally he said dryly, "You'll live," and then, realizing the appositeness of those words, chortled. Tug and Nick continued to look at him uncomfortably.

Nick sat silent, and then said, "You know our class has a big new project. A Memorial Window." And he outlined Wexford's plan.

"That sounds very worthwhile," said Mr. Blackburn. "You say that student over there conceived the idea?"

"Yes. Wexford. Want to meet him?"

•   •   •

Wexford said to A, "If anybody issues from that kitchen carrying a cake with eighteen candles on it and you blokes start bursting into song, I'm going to take the cake and shove it into Mrs. Pete Hallam's face."

"Why her face?"

"Because I don't like her face. Smug. Thinks she's giving the sex-starved little Devon boys a thrill, just by sitting there!"

"About the cake. Aren't we supposed to celebrate your birthday, your coming of age?" inquired B. "Look. For one thing, you can drink liquor legally now, in some states anyway."

Wexford eyed him speculatively. Then he said with elaborate care, "Really?"

Squelched, B nevertheless pressed on. "Anyway, we do have a present for you."

"Oh Lord," said Wexford, rolling his eyes toward the chandelier, "I'll bet it's a wallet!"

"Wide of the mark," said C. "It's this," and he handed him a cashier's check from the local bank, for one hundred dollars, made out to the Memorial Window Fund.

Wexford tilted it this way and that, as though it gave off reflections. Finally he looked up. "Beautiful," he said simply. He winked. "We're on our way."

At that moment the elderly waitress came through the swinging doors of the kitchen bearing a cake with white frosting and eighteen candles. Wexford clenched his teeth fiercely. "You idiots!" he hissed.

" 'Happy birthday to you,' " they began, and as the little ditty progressed, others in the dining room tentatively joined in. Wexford sat tight-shouldered, gripping the table. At the end of the singing there were several voices calling out, inevitably, "Speech, speech!"

He sardonically blew out all the candles and then very slowly and stiffly and with all apparent reluctance rose to his feet.

"I would just like to say," he began in his most urbane, confident tone, "that although as of today I am no longer a child legally, I am still going to be in this child's school for six more months." He paused portentously, and then with a wicked smile added, *"En garde!"* He sat down amid a slightly bewildered smattering of applause.

• • •

"There's a self-possessed boy," remarked Joan Hallam. "Who is he?"

"The editor of the newspaper. There was a big controversy in the paper last term. It looked as though we were going to have riots around here for a while."

"I thought this place was peaceful, just peace and quiet and studies and sports."

He nodded ruefully. "It is, right now."

• • •

"There's something rather impressive about that young man," observed Mr. Blackburn. "I'd like to contribute to that Memorial Window." He got out his wallet and, removing a check from it, made it out in the amount of one hundred dollars. "Here, Tug, take that over to him, with all good wishes."

"The hell with that," murmured Tug. "Wexford!" he called sharply. Getting his attention, he motioned him to come over.

Wexford got up again. He was dressed in his typically conservative gray flannel suit, but violated convention by wearing a Stuart tartan vest underneath. This departure, when added to his longish hair, longish face, and general air of precocious weariness, made him look apart from it all as he ambled across the room to their table.

Introductions were made. Wexford thanked Mr. Blackburn effusively for his contribution. Looking down at Tug, he then said brightly, "Hockey practice must really have been rough. What an eye!" and he stared raptly at it.

Tug shifted in his chair and then said, "Yeah, well some of us at least get out there for sports."

"Mm. And get mixed up at it," Wexford added, chuckling. "You and Cotty Donaldson are on the same side. He's not supposed to give you a shiner." He shook Mr. Blackburn's hand. "Many many thanks again, sir. I hope this will be something you'll be proud to be associated with."

"I'm sure, I'm sure," said Mr. Blackburn.

After he had left, Mr. Blackburn asked, "What is this about Cotty Donaldson? What did he have to do with that black eye? Did he run into you at hockey practice?"

There was a silence and then Tug said, "No, he punched me."

"Did he? Why?"

"Well, because I punched him."

"And why did you do that?"

"Well . . . he pushed me."

"This is beginning to sound very, well, adolescent

to me. He pushed you? I thought he was your best friend up here."

"Well . . . sometimes I guess we see too much of each other, kind of get on each other's nerves. We're cooped up here. You know how it is?" He looked almost pleadingly at his father.

But Mr. Blackburn, Devon '17, had forgotten how it was. Nineteen seventeen had been a long time ago. He recalled a moment on the Fields Beyond, the entire school in phalanx parading toward the Stadium for the climactic football game of the season, with the entire student body of the archrival, Conover, ranged opposite them, banners flying in the stiff autumnal wind, and they had cheered in unison each other's Headmaster, except that the Conover boys had roared, "Fairy! Fairy! Fairy! Fairy!" for Headmaster Carey, and the Devonians had hissed back, "Feuissssssss!" for Headmaster Feuiss. That was as close to open hostility as they had come. Apart from that, he recalled drowsing in steamy classrooms, and his head bent over a book at a desk opposite his roommate's in the evening, running track, and numerous jolly vacations. Cooped up? He couldn't recall feeling that. He said so to Tug.

"Oh well," said Tug, his face suggesting that hopelessness of it all.

"That young man Wexford there," went on Mr. Blackburn. "That's somebody you could do well to see a lot of, not just the athletes. He's going places."

• • •

"You never talk about the war," said Joan Hallam over coffee. "Do you think you should keep it bottled up? I know it must have been a horrible ordeal. Especially being captured, made a prisoner. But then getting away and having the Partisans help you and escaping! Why don't you ever talk about it?"

He looked at her and then muttered, "Because it was miserable and I was scared sh— out of my mind a lot of the time, and now I want to try to begin to forget it." He took a forkful of apple pie à la mode. "Would you want to talk about it if you'd had cancer and—no, that isn't a good comparison. I don't think there is a good comparison. In prison camp there is just one thought. Food. That's all anybody could ever think about. I took all the risks of breaking out of that camp not to be free really but to have the chance of a square meal again. That escape just kind of happened as far as I was concerned, and everything else just happened—out of my hands—and now it's over and somehow I'm here at Devon having dinner, which I wasn't quite able to finish—how amazing—I left some food on my plate."

"Having dinner with your ex-wife who deserted you."

He made a deprecating face.

"I wouldn't mind, you know," she went on, "I mean I could—if you ever wanted to—you see at that time I was so damned confused—and if you thought we could—"

He just shook his head. "It's down the drain, honey," he said quietly. "It went down the drain to the sewer with the other shit and now it's out to sea."

9

The winter of 1945–46, like all winters in New Hampshire, gave the impression for long months of being interminable, nature's permanent state, the Great Frost. Ultimately in early April it began to break up and dwindle away. Certain intimations of green came into bushes and shrubbery alongside the solid red-brick buildings of the school. The stands of timber beyond the Playing Fields acquired a suggestion of future fullness and a sheen of grassiness lay thinly on the fields themselves. The chilly air began to lose its authority; the little Devon River was full of icy water sliding swiftly from inland snowfields, pitching over the miniature dam in the center of the town and mingling with the wide, tidewater Naguamsett River and on to the ocean.

The Memorial Window was already in place. A distinguished elderly artist in Maine had been given the commission and had executed it swiftly, even hurriedly. Enthusiasm for war memorials and the money to pay for them could evaporate quickly in peacetime, he remembered from 1919 to 1920. So the completed stained-glass panels had been brought by truck to the school in the middle of March, installed in the Chapel during the short vacation at the end of the month, and were ready for dedication on the first Sunday of the new term.

Almost everyone agreed at once that here was the kind of window which suited the neo-Gothic architecture of the Chapel in general, and the artistic taste, or lack of it, prevailing at the Devon School.

Devon was traditionally not interested in any of the arts except literature and music. The arts of painting and sculpture were assumed to be carried on in Paris and Greenwich Village, where they probably should stay. When a work of graphic art was required, as in the case of the Memorial Window, then two or three very conservative figures in the art world in Boston were consulted, and their advice followed.

The result was now in place behind the altar in the chancel. It was about fifteen feet high, arching to a Gothic point. In severe lettering at the bottom was printed:

PRESENTED BY THE CLASS OF 1946
IN HONOR OF THOSE DEVONIANS
WHO SERVED AND SACRIFICED
1941–1945.

It was a representational work, but not slavishly so. An airman, a soldier, and a sailor could be discerned along with what might be artillery pieces, objects—fighter planes, hawks?—flying through gray-white clouds, a ship's prow or else a shark's fin in a blue-green sea, a swatch which might portray a tropical beach, and a large white stylized dove spreading its wings toward the top of the window, a dove which the Roman Catholic and High Episcopal elements in the school might interpret as an angel.

The major figures and shapes were so organized as to form an unobtrusive but discernable V, as in Victory.

Pete Hallam moved quietly to a seat at the very

back of the rows of pews in the little west transept reserved for the faculty. He had a heavy cold and had dosed himself with cough medicine, which didn't seem to be doing much good. If he started coughing in the middle of the service, he would leave.

From his seat the altar but not the window behind it could be seen. As the organ played a Bach fugue, with students and faculty making their way to their places, Pete walked forward to have a look at it.

He liked the colors: blues and greens, grayish white, golden yellow.

It was impressive in its way, it was dignified, it defied any idea of mocking it, and to him it was simply a lie. There was much too much nobility and there was a total absence of boredom. Well, how did you portray boredom in stained glass? There was a lack of pain, and a void where monumental irritation ought to be. The very beauty of the window, totally at odds with the abject physical ugliness of military life, was a lie. This window depicted something grace- ful and exalted and clean and beautiful. It was as though a tornado were portrayed as lively, quick- sand as sport.

He pulled his eyes in disgust away from it and walked back to his seat.

"Splendid, isn't it?" said Roscoe Latch.

Pete knew Roscoe to be a brilliant and normally shrewd man. This praise was genuine. How could he be so wrong? War must be a fever, a sickness, a pain you evidently had to experience in order to understand. If you hadn't been there you couldn't be expected to have any real idea of it, whether you were brilliant and shrewd or stupid and a fool.

The reason for this occurred to him now: the expe- rience of being actively involved in fighting a war was so wretched that people not so involved, no matter how sympathetic and concerned and suspense- filled and patriotic, were not willing to go through it, even in their imagination. Some had the imagination to do it. But they wouldn't. That was asking too much.

Pete had to make some reply to Roscoe. "It's—uh—impressive, that it is."

Roscoe's shining, slightly mad eyes gazed at him. "You don't like it." He continued gazing, and Pete returned his stare unblinkingly. "To you it's a fake," Roscoe went on in his hooting voice. "Well . . . it *is* suitable here."

"There I can agree with you."

The service began with a burst of martial, stirring organ music, and after that there would be a hymn. Pete felt himself involuntarily tensing. Would it be, were they really going to . . . Yes, they were. Oh yes.

●   ●   ●

"Onward Christian Soldiers"
  Then the choir sang
  "For Those in Peril on the Sea"
  Then they sang
  "Now Thank We All Our God"

●   ●   ●

It was stirring. Even Pete was stirred a little. A good male chorus, a fine organ, and those hymns were basically stirring. This is good theater, he thought.

If only this service in this handsome miniature Gothic cathedral with this music and this window *did* have something to do with the Second World War. If only the war had been anything like this.

Instead, his mind unwillingly went back to recall what serving in the Infantry had really been like. It boiled down simply to physical exhaustion, unutterable fatigue, just as prison camp had been hunger. During the campaign in Italy he continually thought of a movie he had seen before the war, *Things to Come*, based on a futuristic novel by H. G. Wells. In

that future there had been a plague of Wandering
Sickness, and his mind continually had the recollection from this movie of gaunt staggering human
shapes, zombies walking in a trance of undead empty
horror. That had been the Infantry.

> God of our Fathers,
> Whose almighty hand
> Leads forth in beauty
> All the starry band.
>
> Of shining worlds
> In splendor through the skies
> Our grateful song
> Before Thy throne arise.

Then came the sermon. The Rev. Stephen Farnum
Rodd, "Steve" as he liked to be called by everybody
including the students and the cleaning women, spoke
very well and eloquently and from his heart, but it
was a heart which had never been stopped by an
explosion next to his feet, an explosion which might
castrate him or take a leg away.

Wexford then stepped into the pulpit to speak for
the Class of 1946. He at least made a certain kind of
sense. The gist was that his class had had no part in
winning the war but was ready to dedicate itself to
guarding the victory won by their heroic predeces-
sors. The word "heroic" would normally have grated
on Pete, but Wexford enunciated it with a certain
irony, it seemed to him.

This young man was a rare one, all right. Pete
wondered what someone like that would wind up
doing with himself in this life. What happened to
you when at age eighteen you were moneyed, bright,
articulate, charming, meretricious, domineering, hyp-
ocritical, underhanded, and an egomaniac?

Conceivably Wexford, alone among the students,

might dimly sense what they were really here for today. They were memorializing young men who had lost their youth or their lives confining a disaster caused by others.

Triumphant chords rose once again from the organ. The service had begun with "Onward Christian Soldiers." Were they really going to conclude it with . . . did they have that much gall or confidence or blindness? Indeed they did. Over the towering chords of the organ soared the voices of the choir:

Hal-le-lu-jah!
For the Lord God Omnipotent reigneth.

Into Pete's rattled and fundamentally outraged mind the last word slithered: Reigneth. Raineth. Rain. Italian rain. It had poured down like some Old Testament curse upon them for months, muddying every slogging footstep, making clammy every corner where they tried to rest or, God willing, sleep a little, depressing every view, every thought. For the Lord God Omnipotent raineth and raineth and raineth, that season in war-soaked Italy.

As he emerged into the wintry sunshine Pete abruptly began to cough again; his cold reactivated itself. Not once had he coughed during the dedicatory service. He had been, to a certain degree, hypnotized by what he had seen and heard and remembered there.

On the steps in front of the Chapel the Headmaster's wife went up to congratulate the artist, Eeno Radnot, who looked rather like Albert Einstein, and Wexford, who today radiated a certain resemblance to Tyrone Power.

"It's quite perfect," she said. And then she burst into tears.

In a society as reflexively understated in word and deed as Devon's, these words and those tears placed

an unbreakable seal of approval on the window.
Mrs. Wherry had called it perfect. Perfect! And she
had cried. Cried!

•   •   •

Spring, once having forced itself through the massive dead weight of winter, came on irresistibly;
yellow bursts of forsythia suddenly appeared everywhere, and one or two people maintained that the
flowers almost matched the golden yellow in the
Memorial Window. The lacrosse players hammered
up and down the Playing Fields, the sharp whack of
a well-hit baseball and thudding soccer kicks broke
on the spring air. Crew shells skimmed with their
thin oars like huge delicate water bugs across the
shining water of the Naguamsett. Practical-joke season was here and two members of the mountain-
climbing team were discovered at seven o'clock one
morning busily belaying up the sheer four-story exterior of the Library. The Dean was for the first time in
living memory so overcome by the daring of this
violation of all rules and so relieved at the safe and
skillful climb that he did not expel them, did not
place them on probation, but gave them a severe
warning muted by the visible effort his Old Proph-
et's face was making to keep from breaking into a
grin.

Devon beat the Harvard freshmen at baseball.

Pete Hallam knew that there was a certain breed
of skier who would pursue snow to the highest
mountain fields in the remotest country far into spring
if there was a possibility of skiing on it.

Such a possibility, indeed a certainty, existed at
Tuckerman's Ravine on Mount Washington in northern New Hampshire. So Friday afternoon in the
middle of April he, the Blackburn boys and the rest
of the ski group set out in his station wagon, heading north.

They went straight to bed in the lodge at the foot

of the mountain that night so as to be able to get up at dawn and climb the mountain to the ravine, carrying food and sleeping bags in their packs.

It was one of those brisk, cold mornings in the north country when the mountain air seemed baptismally cleansing, unstained by the least trace of foreign matter, infused with a thin purity which promised permanent health and vigor and life.

"Do you know what I think?" said Pete Hallam between breaths as he led the group toiling up the rugged trail carrying their packs, skis, poles and boots. "I think you're all a bunch of sissies."

"You do, do you?" responded Tug. "What do we have to do to get to be he-men, like you? Go to war and get shot up?"

Pete emitted one short barking laugh. It was the first time a reference to war and its ordeals had brought out anything but grimness in him.

"Well maybe you don't have to go that far," he conceded.

"What do we have to do?"

"Carry my pack!" he groaned.

All of the boys were thrown into a quandary by this reply. They had always thought of Pete as one of those leaders who did more than the least of his men. He might be expected to carry one or two of their packs, but surrender his own? Never. On the other hand, there was his damaged leg. To offer to take his pack or not to offer to take his pack?

"Pass it back to me," said Tug shortly.

"Just kidding," replied Pete.

"Tell us about the war," goaded Nick. "Is that where you discovered you were a Leader of Men?"

"Yeah," said Pete. "Now if I could just find some somewhere. And now, shut up, save your breath. This is a longish climb."

They toiled upward along the broken trail.

To those who had never seen it, such as Nick

Blackburn, Tuckerman's Ravine was on the unbe-
lievable side, with an unacceptably steep sheet of
icy-looking snow called the Headwall. It began at
the crest of the mountain and some distance below
formed a lip over a ledge which could only be nego-
tiated on the downward run by a long leap into
space and landing on the steep sheet of ice-snow
and hurtling onto the runout.

"We're supposed to ski *this*?" queried Nick in an
incredulous tone.

"Sure," said Tug unconvincingly. "Over the Lip.
You aren't a skier until you've done it."

"I'm not a skier," replied Nick immediately.

"You are, you are. Listen. It's easy. Well, it isn't
easy, but it's possible. People have done it."

"People have swum the English Channel too."

"Are you chicken?"

"Yes."

Tug looked with amusement at him. "I believe I
am too," he then said calmly. "This isn't—the way it
was described—this isn't the way I pictured it."

There were two or three other groups of skiers in
the big steep half-bowl formed by the Headwall.
One of these groups was already plodding single file
upward along one side of the Headwall, carrying
their skis. Beneath the Lip they adjusted their bindings and one by one proceeded down. The first skier
ventured to aim his skis downward with the greatest
caution, gained speed swiftly, tried a stem christie,
failed, desperately threw himself into a snowplow—
hopeless, and falling on his face proceeded spread-
eagle to slide all the way to the bottom. It was clear
that one mistake and you were out on the Headwall.
The next two skiers headed downward with more
style and more confidence, checking regularly, and
reached the bottom safely.

Nick followed this feat with a fixed stare. "Well,"
he remarked, "that's some skiing."

"That ain't nothin'," said Tug, pulling on his lined leather gloves. "Just suppose instead of starting below the Lip he started above it, at the crest, and he gets going real fast, comes to the Lip, dives head-and-tips-first into space, lands like a feather going—I don't know—sixty miles an hour on that steepest part there and then barrels to the finish."

"Um-hum," grunted Nick noncommittally.

"What would you think of that?"

"I'd think the little men in white with the nets would come and catch the guy."

"Lots of skiers have done it."

"How did they come out of it?"

"Oh, the odd broken leg, a few concussions. You know."

"Any corpses?"

"I don't think anybody's actually been killed going over the Lip, not yet anyway. Have they, Pete?"

"Not that I know of."

"I wonder why they do it?" said Nick, looking at Pete.

Pete was silent, and then said, "Because they're bored. Some people can't live without, well, you might say terror. They don't feel alive without it. In the end, they'd rather be dead than bored. They do that when they're twenty. When they're forty, if they last that long, they're often drunks, I believe."

"What gets into them?" Nick asked.

Pete looked up at the steep bowl above them, sheer challenge. "Destruction can be beautiful," he said, "to some people. Don't ask me why. It just is. And if they can't find anything else to destroy, then they just destroy themselves." He surveyed his group; everybody looked ready, booted, black ski pants, sweaters over turtleneck pullovers, leather mittens, tinted goggles on their foreheads in case the sun came out, all dressed pretty much alike, conformists— the very last thing they would have admitted about themselves—boys in their late teens who wanted to be raging rebels and individualists, just as long as they were like the other guys. They were ready to pick up their skis and poles and start the climb, but seemed a little reluctant to show that they were, glancing guardedly now and then at the Headwall.

"Why does it look *bigger* than I remember it?" complained R.T. "This is the third time I've been here. The damn thing *grows*, I tell you."

"Maybe you've shrunk," suggested Chet.

"That's it! I've shrunk. I can feel it. Right now, I'm shrinking." Then, in a mock little-child's voice, "I'm too tiny to go up on that great big mounting!"

"Pick up your skis, you great lummox," ordered Pete. "Let's go."

They started to tramp toward the Headwall, unfamiliar warning aches abruptly stirring in their legs and backs. Reaching the point where it began to curve upward, they dug their boots into the broken snow trail at the side of the bowl, climbing ever more steeply upward, coming finally to the top of the Headwall, beneath the ledge and the Lip.

Nick, adjusting his bindings, thought that looking down over the Headwall from this lower position was by itself the scariest-looking slope he had yet confronted: a sheer precipitous sheet of ice-snow, like a giant white chute, offering no grip, no stopping place, no mound to check against, nothing, just a diving incline of slipperiest challenge.

The least accomplished skier should go first, he reasoned, remembering the group they had just seen. "Bye-bye," he called out, and forcing himself to lean forward into the fall line instead of backward away from it, he began plummeting downward, came up off his skis to turn—*made* it—traversed briefly—up and down again—another turn; he switched back and forth several times until toward the bottom the surface was so ideally smooth that he risked a long sweeping turn which went perfectly until he caught an edge and he was instantly down on his side, rapidly sliding the remaining distance to the bottom.

Nuts. But even with the fall at the end, the run had been so exhilarating, such a thrill, he had done so damn well except for the one split second when his left ski wasn't angled just exactly right, that he was pleased with himself. He had skied the Headwall, and he had skied it, almost all of it, damn well. In fact, it was the best bit of skiing he had ever done. Something about the danger had made him better.

The others followed along behind him, and once having made it down all of them gained confidence and made several more runs before stopping in the early afternoon for coffee from a Thermos bottle, and sandwiches. After a rest they then started up once more, calculating that the sun was still high enough for at least one more run.

When they reached the top of the Headwall beneath the Lip, Tug said, "I'm going on up," not even breaking stride.

"Tug," said Pete.

Tug stopped. "Yeah?"

"Maybe you shouldn't try it this trip."

"Why not? It's the end of the season. I'm in shape. Legs are good. Earlier in the season I wouldn't have been ready. But now I am." He paused, squinting.

Pete looked at him. It would have been safer for Pete, as well as for Tug, to forbid the run over the Lip. If he was injured, Pete, who had taken it upon himself to be responsible for this unofficial, unorganized team, would be held at fault.

It was clear that Tug wanted to try it today. "Go on then," said Pete. "Have you figured out how you're going to take it?"

"Yes."

Tug, skis on his shoulder, poles dangling from his hand, continued alone up the steep white sheet of snow, unbroken here because no one had ventured to ski over the Lip since the last snowfall.

"You guys," began Pete, "go on and ski to the bottom. I'll stay here. When Tug comes over the Lip I'll start down too, so I'll be close behind him."

Nick and the others skied down, Nick finding the Headwall practically a cinch now that Tug was going to attempt something so much riskier. Beneath his eyes and his skis this steep, slippery bowl diminished quickly to just another slope where you had to pay attention and not do anything foolish. The peril had risen off it and gone up over the curving overhang of the Lip.

At the bottom they stopped at the end of the short runout and turned their eyes upward over the ledge to the top of the Headwall, where Pete could be seen standing quietly; they looked on up past the line of the ledge to the swelling curve of the Lip, to the tiny figure just reaching the crest, Tug with his skis.

There were clusters of clouds moving across the sky with patches of blue among them. As the occasional openings passed, the sun's rays poured dazzlingly down on the Ravine. The big bowl was overcast, in a somber grayish light. Tug's minute shape at the crest of the icy bowl was set against a patch of blue behind him. He looked overwhelmed by the massiveness of the mountain beneath him, the limitless sky above and behind. Below him spread the steep bowl, Pete's lone figure at the top of it, the line of the ledge, the swelling shape of the Lip, and finally, against that elemental sky, the minuscule, ridiculous little animated figure preparing to hurtle itself downward, Tugwell Blackburn.

"I kind of wish one of us had gone up there and come down with him," said R.T. uncertainly.

"To tell you the truth," said Cotty, "I just don't feel up to it myself. Just haven't got it today. Maybe next year or . . ."

"I should have gone," said Nick.

"You? You couldn't go over the Lip. You'd kill yourself."

Nick knew that and it confused him.

"Pete would have gone," put in Chet, "except for his leg."

"Of course."

"Anyway," observed Guy, always logical, "what difference except psychologically does it make if one of us was with him there now? We can't come *down* with him, holding hands, can we? He's got to make the run and take the chances alone, no matter what."

"It's like life," said Nick with a nervous laugh. "Alone, alone," he intoned with mock portentousness, "we face it all alone."

"You're beginning to babble."

"I *am* babbling. I want to babble."

"I think he's getting ready to start down," said Cotty edgily.

The other group of skiers, who were on the trail upward alongside the Headwall, all halted where they were to look up at the little figure outlined between the field of the snow at his feet and the vivid patch of depthless blue sky behind him.

Maybe this is why he's doing it, thought Nick suddenly. He's got the world, this little world here, watching him. Maybe that's part of it. And the rest? He thought of what Pete had said. Is he using terror to keep away boredom? Does he have to try to destroy something? Even as a last resort, himself?

The little figure started moving downward. How strange, Nick's mind registered, that we can't hear anything, the hiss of his skis on the snow, the whip of the wind going past. At that instant a cloud drifted away and the full dazzle of the sun glittered on the wide fields of snow. It was as though Tug were part of a silent movie, as fake as the Keystone Kops, and just as free of real danger.

Moving faster, but checking as he came, he approached the swelling hump of the Lip, leaped out from it, hurled soundlessly into space; there was an eternal moment and then he hit the steep icy plummet of the Headwall. Pete was skiing down behind him, Tug was tearing downward triumphantly, they began to cheer and then Tug, trying to check, lurched sideways. A ski snapped off as he went flailing and sliding downward.

When they got to him he was lying in the snow. Pete had removed his other ski, and was methodically feeling his arms and legs. "Left knee," mumbled Tug, "twisted pretty bad, I think."

Pete examined it with his hands as gently as possible while Tug writhed. Tug looked vaguely up at the others. "You were great," said R.T.

"It looked terrific," burst out Nick. "Just that little thing at the end. Like me. I—"

"How do you mean, like you?" asked Tug, looking opaquely up at him.

"I did the same thing on my run, my first run. Beautiful until the very end and then I caught an edge. Anyway, you *did it*. Over the Lip. You're a skier!"

The others joined in with enthusiasm.

"I don't know about this place," murmured Tug.

After Pete had determined that there were no broken bones, they helped him to his feet. Guy, who had gone to retrieve the other ski at the end of the runout, returned with it.

"These mountains," said Tug, "how long do they go on?"

"Go on?" said Nick, who was supporting him under his shoulder, helping him toward a log shelter at the end of the runout. "They go on into Vermont—you know that—and on I don't know into New York State too, I guess. Why?"

"Does my knee ever hurt!"

"Nothing's broken. You just gave it a bad twist."

"You can see a lot of mountains from up there," Tug rambled on.

"I'll bet," said Nick. "Must be a great view from up there."

"I don't know if it was Vermont I was seeing."

"Probably not. Just more New Hampshire."

"Could we put some hot water on my knee?"

"I don't know where we could get any hot water up here," replied Nick, helping Tug up the single step into the log shelter, and sitting down on a bench.

"There're mountains everywhere," observed Tug. "We've got 'em at home."

"That's right," agreed Nick, looking into his face. "What went wrong at the end of your run? Boy, what a beautiful trip you had up to that! Over the Lip. Fan-*tas*-tic. You flew through the air like a champion. How'd it feel?"

Tug looked vaguely at him and then was silent, lightly passing his hand over his knee.

The others came to the shelter. There was a conference out of Tug's hearing. Pete said that obviously Tug could not hike to the bottom of the mountain, that in any case they had planned to sleep out up here tonight and were equipped for it. The other group of skiers were now preparing to go down the mountain and would arrange for transportation, a Jeep or heavy truck, to break its way up the still officially closed Auto Road and carry Tug and the rest of them down. But that would be impossible until tomorrow. Tug, aside from a badly twisted knee, which might or might not be very serious, could in either case spend a night on the mountain without risk. He would just be very uncomfortable. Pete had some aspirin and that might help some.

Nick got the aspirin and a glass of water and walked over to Tug. The others began to gather wood to build a fire for the supper, beans and frank-furters. Coca-Cola bottles had been buried in the snow.

Tug took down his ski pants and they examined his knee. It was becoming swollen and discolored, and very painful to touch. "It burns," he murmured, pulling up his pants again.

"The aspirin will help in a minute. How scared were you going over the Lip? *Of course* you were scared. But how much? A little, a lot, or out of your mind?"

"Out of your mind," echoed Tug.

"Hm? You were?"

"I was what?"

"Scared. Out of your mind?"

Tug frowned. "I know there's homework. I know I've got some homework to do. For tomorrow. But what is it?" He turned to look at Nick. "Do you know what it is?"

"Tomorrow's Sunday. You don't have any home-work due tomorrow."

"Oh." Tug lapsed into silence, rubbing his thigh above the injured knee.

"I know you've done a little ski-jumping before, but I'll bet that's the longest jump you ever made. You really leaned into it. What a great feeling when you landed!"

"The mountain threw me off. I got bounced right off the Lip."

"Hey, that's pretty good, almost like poetry in a way."

The sun had disappeared behind the crest above Tuckerman's Ravine and a brisk, chilly wind with still a hint of winter's ferocity swept roughly through. The high-reaching evergreens bent and moaned. It was brought home to them that they were alone on the mountain.

"Why don't you go and lie down in your sleeping

bag?'' suggested Nick. "Wait. I'll go and get it and put it in here. Just stay there."

Tug stared in front of him. Nick walked over to where they had left their packs, and came back with Tug's sleeping bag. The Ravine was sinking into a pool of chilly darkness, while above them the sky still glowed in the last long rays of the sun.

"It's kind of weird up here, isn't it," said Nick, spreading out the sleeping bag in front of Tug. "The sun's still shining up there, and here we are with darkness all around, down here in the woods. There's a strangeness about it."

Tug turned with an almost painful effort to look up at the crest of the Ravine and the still-glowing sky. "It's all bright up there," he said slowly. "Bright from the snow and you can see the other states. Maybe I should have stayed up there, where it's bright and you can see everything."

"Naw. You want to be down here with us."

"Where is everybody? Who's with us?"

"The usual gang, they're over there getting something to eat ready. You hungry?"

"What?"

"I said, are you hungry?"

"Yeah, but what'd you say just before that?"

"I don't know, nothing much. About the top of the mountain still in sunlight and—"

"Was I—how'd I get down?"

"Tug, listen, get out of your pants and that sweater—you've got long underwear on—get in this sleeping bag. I'll get you some . . . well, all we've got is beans and frankfurters. You can rest."

"There were all these ranges of mountains I could see in the glare. First it was hazy up there and then all of a sudden the snow came up bright, blazing, like jewelry or fires or something, it just turned on all of a sudden around me—like footlights—blazing up all around me, and those ranges I could see off in the distance . . . and then the mountain swelled up and it threw me off into space and I was flying. I guess you don't believe that." He sucked in some air. "No mountain underneath me because it threw me off. I don't know." He shook his head vigorously. "I can't remember too much. Who's with us up here?"

"Pete. The usual gang."

"Pete," he repeated vaguely. "How'd I get off the crest with all the footlights blazing around me? Did I jump? Oh, that's right, I got thrown off, out into space."

"Let's get you out of those pants and sweater and you can lie down and rest."

Pete and the others were coming toward the shelter carrying paper plates with frankfurters and beans, and bottles of Coke. They sat around and ate, the conversation desultory as everyone glanced apprehensively from time to time at Tug, who sat silent and apathetic, moving the beans around his plate with a fork. "Eat your frankfurter," said Nick. Tug with difficulty broke off a piece of frankfurter and speared it with his fork. Then he forgot to put it in his mouth.

"What's the difference between frankfurters and hot dogs?" asked Guy.

"Frankfurters are German and hot dogs are American," answered Pete.

"Pretty unpatriotic, us eating Kraut food," observed Cotty. "And on Mount *Washington*."

"If only Hochschwender were here," put in R.T. "He'd be happy with us at last."

The conversation straggled on in the darkness, the fire fitfully flickering nearby. Then they all hauled out their sleeping bags and prepared to bed down for the night. Nick and Pete spread theirs in the shelter near Tug's.

The evening's gusts had died down, and a still,

starry night emerged over the mountain, a beautiful
spread of nighttime glitter in the blackness. The tall,
slender evergreens stood silent, sentinels in the night;
after a while a half-formed moon slid over the crest
of the Ravine, and the great slab of the Headwall
acquired a spectral, ashen glow, as though it were
an hallucination or a dream, insubstantial as a cloud.

• • • •

Tug Blackburn lay in his sleeping bag; he held the
front of it tightly up under his chin. It had become
quite cold on the mountain, but it was snug and
warm inside the sleeping bag. The real numbing
chill had clamped itself upon his mind: I can't really
remember anything, he confided to himself tersely, I
can't get anything straight in my head. Who is that
shape lying over there? Some kind of mountain ani-
mal? Or is it Nick?

Or isn't it? If I move in this sleeping bag the
hissing sound of it will be so loud it will break all
over this mountain. Sudden loud noises in the mountains are what cause avalanches. That great field of
snow hanging just above us up there: it could come
loose and rush and roll down on us, thunder down
on us lying here, we're helpless here, everybody
asleep but me, if there is anybody else, if I'm not
alone up here. Any second that huge field of snow
may come loose and bury me alive. I'd never be
found. The snow never melts up here. Wherever up
here is.

How old am I? Is that my brother or a mountain
lion?

I'm going completely crazy—out of my mind—and
I will be locked up in the Funny Farm and rot there
for the rest of my life. My brother *was* here a while
ago and I could tell from the way he was looking at
me that he knows I'm now completely crazy. The
Funny Farm, what a place to end up. Why didn't I
join the Army and get killed usefully someplace,

instead of winding up in a miserable lunatic asylum? If there was a cliff somewhere I'd jump off it and end it all right now. End it all, end it all. My God, it's come to thinking like that.

My mind's broken, leg too, Tug told himself tensely. "Broken!" he cried out. Pete, in his sleeping bag, abruptly turned to look across at him. "God, God," Tug raved on, "broken. It *must be* broken. Oh God, oh holy mother the Church. Oh-h-h," he groaned, and then fell silent. In his sleeping bag Pete very gradually relaxed and tried to go back to sleep.

Tug's feverish inner monologue continued. Jump off—something—the white glitter of the snow as those footlights suddenly came up, blinding my eyes and I just had to lunge into the empty space, the mountain shrugged and blinded me and I took a wild dive into the endless space beyond the swell of the Lip and I knew the mountain would not be below to support me when I came down, I had gone too far, taking the dare to go up alone to the crest and look around me as though I was the ruler of this mountain and all the ranges off as far as I could see toward Virginia or North Carolina or wherever it is, and I felt I was the King of the Mountain, this mountain and all the other mountains, and that was an evil thought and so the mountain itself just gave a shake and blazed up those lights to blind me and I spun off into space and now I'm still falling and there is nothing *nothing* to ever catch me and my mind is gone and my connection with everything has been broken and that's not my brother that's a mountain lion ready to spring.

10

The grounds of the Devon School, optimistically green with early grass and budding trees, had a cloistral purity about them very early Monday morning when Pete Hallam came out of his quarters in Pembroke House for his daily run. The muscles in his shrapnel-gouged left leg would eventually come back somewhere near normal, the doctors thought, if he unremittingly exercised them, every day, for the rest of his life. If he neglected them for even relatively short periods, they could begin to deteriorate rapidly.

In running shoes, gray sweat suit with a towel around his neck, Pete began to trot along Front Street where it passed between two large sweeps of lawn, with the Headmaster's House, a muddled, homey nineteenth-century pile behind one lawn, and the red-brick First Academy Building behind the other. Beyond these two structures rose the white granite miniature cathedral, the Devon Chapel, its rose-windowed façade glowing down on the campus in the early morning sunlight.

Off a little on the right was the Infirmary, where they had taken Tug Blackburn immediately on returning from Mount Washington. The attendant nurse had summoned Dr. Stanpole, and Dr. Stanpole had, after his examination and hearing the fact of Tug's jump and fall, concluded that he was suffering from a concussion of the brain, "probably a mild one," and had had him put immediately to bed. Later today Pete would go over and see him.

The matchlessly pure air of this wood-surrounded, tidewater New England village pumping in and out of his lungs suffused him with that feeling of fresh drive and energy he had thought gone from him forever along the muddy tracks of Italy, something he had felt as a student here, that life probably could last forever. If you just kept trotting along these streets and across these fields and through these woods then probably you gradually metamorphosed into the Great God Pan, hooved and the soul of mischief, and lurked here forever, causing trouble.

Not that anything Greek was needed here for that. If you had seven hundred isolated young men you had an absolute mathematical certainty to have trouble.

There was Tug Blackburn on the Headwall. It had simply been unavoidable for him to take the challenge of going over the Lip. Had Pete forbidden it Tug would have by hook or crook gotten himself back to Mount Washington the next weekend and done it then. Better to say yes to the inevitable than to say no and have it done behind your back, with maybe nobody around to cope with an emergency.

Of course Mr. Blackburn, father and financial benefactor, might not see it that way. He might look askance at Pete for allowing his son to run that risk—to end up with a concussion of the brain; he might be outraged, he might yell and shout and write letters. Well, as they said, that was the way the ball bounced sometimes, and T.S., Tough Shit.

Pete trotted up to the Chapel. His left leg hurt, of course, it virtually always hurt, he could feel the holes where the muscle used to be, but he had grown as used to it as feeling his tongue in his mouth.

Fresh young grass was coming up in the precincts around the Chapel and Pete began to circle the building on the brick walk through the grass.

In front of him he then noticed shards of broken glass, colored broken glass. His first thought was that sloppy workmen had left some extra bits and pieces here after installing the Memorial Window.

He looked up and saw a gaping vacuity where the Memorial Window had been. It had been smashed out of its framing, and only jagged edges of glass still clung to the frame here and there. Parts of the dedicatory lettering at the bottom remained like the broken teeth in a has-been boxer:

WH VED RIF 9 4

Pete stood still, balancing. There hadn't been any wild windstorm; no flailing tree branch had broken it. Somebody had come here overnight and smashed it to bits.

•   •   •

I think I'd better see Tug Blackburn, flashed into his mind as he stood there in a state of vague stunned perplexity, I think I'd better see him first. Those words Tug had cried out in his delirium—"It must be broken . . . the church." Pete felt a slow chill at the back of his neck. Tug had always been one of those especially gentle strong boys, yet he had fought with Cotty. And now had his concussion allowed the violence to escape in a more irrational and destructive way?

Pete headed for the Infirmary, carefully picking his way through the shattered glass in a quixotic attempt to keep from breaking the breakage. He was shaken by this shattered window. Then he was amazed at himself for being shaken. After all, what had happened? Some colored glass had been broken. When he let some images from the Italian campaign move like slides before his mind's eye—an arm suddenly turned into bloody ganglia, a face smashed, a belly blown away—the triviality before him was obvious. Even when it came to the destruction of buildings, the picture of the monumental and venerable majesty of Monte Cassino Monastery reduced to a meaningless mount of rubble, then these shards of broken glass, like the missing bits of his leg, shrank to the scale of negligible details.

But the window would not remain so. That jagged vacancy behind the Chapel altar shocked him again. Other Devonian images sprang before him: Wexford urbanely proud of himself at the dedicatory service; Dr. Wherry's wife's sudden tears; the almost melodramatic sneer he had seen so often on Hochschwender's face; Tug Blackburn's vacant eyes at the bottom of the Headwall; the Pembroke Boys slouched in the chairs in the Butt Room, talking over their innate hostility toward Eric Hochschwender, and laughing it away, that time.

Coming around the other side of the Chapel he started down the short lane to the Infirmary. He felt the hole in his leg; the skin seemed to be stretched there too tightly; it would always be too tight, always ache; the leg would always be rather weak, whatever the morale-boosting official opinion of the doctors might be.

At the Infirmary the nurse, Mrs. Quimby, was surprised to see such an early caller, but she was not going to say anything about visiting hours to Pete Hallam. Mr. Peter Hallam of the History and Physical Education Departments was the Fair-Haired Master of the Devon School, their very own Wounded Athlete Veteran Prisoner of War Who Had Escaped. He watched with interest as she swiftly abrogated several rules for him.

"The doctor hasn't been here yet today," she said, smiling. "In fact, he's never here this early. But of course you go right ahead up and see Tugwell. We put him in the room at the top of the stairs, first on the left." Pete started up. "He's awake," she added mechanically, as an afterthought.

A burst of enraged laughter swelled up in Pete, which he was barely able to suppress. He's awake! *Of course* he's awake! This is a hospital. You are a nurse. I have been wounded and was hospitalized for quite a while. Do you suppose *I* don't know he's awake! If you'd said "He's asleep," then that would have amazed me.

At the door Pete knocked. "Come in," said Tug blearily.

He was lying in a hospital bed next to a window which looked down across a lawn to the Center Common and its red-brick classroom buildings. An uneaten breakfast sat on a bed tray. Tug's usual brisk alertness remained in a state of blurred vagueness.

"Ah . . . hi," he said blinking at him. "I didn't . . . I uh . . . funny seeing you here. Did you get hurt too?"

"No." Pete stood next to the bed, looking down. "Don't you remember Saturday yet?"

"Sort of. Some of it. I . . . uh . . . went over the Lip, didn't I. Guess I banged my head. I don't remember that at all."

"How do you feel otherwise?"

"Sore. Every muscle. Headache. Scared."

"What of?" asked Pete, crossing to sit down in a straight chair.

Tug opened his eyes more widely: somehow that reassured Pete. He had begun to fear that the foggy, low-lidded look had settled on Tug for good. "Scared of being the only shell-shocked victim of World War Two who never heard a shot."

"Ha," laughed Pete mechanically, watching him.

"Why are you . . . um, here, anyway?" Tug struggled to look out through the window. Students were hurrying up the lane outside toward the morning Chapel service.

"I wanted to tell you something before anyone else got to you. I just, well, felt I wanted to tell you." And see your reaction, Pete added to himself. "Last night somebody busted the Memorial Window. Completely destroyed it."

Tug looked at him at length. Then he frowned and said, "I see," very calmly. "You think I did it, because I'm nuts."

Pete's face showed no reaction for a moment. Then he said quietly, "I don't see how you could have. You're here—"

"I can walk. And nothing would be easier than slipping out of this place in the middle of the night."

"All the glass seemed to be outside. As though it was smashed by somebody from the inside."

Tug's face became locked into a puzzled, mystified expression Pete could never have imagined on it. Then Tug said, "I'm on the Devon Council, remember? I've got keys to the Chapel."

They stared at each other for a while and then Pete asked quietly, "Did you break the window, Tug?"

Tug looked across at him with an odd, pleading expression on his face. Then he said helplessly, "I just don't know. Can you beat that? I don't know."

• • •

The students and faculty were converging on the Chapel for the daily service. Then swiftly the word spread across the campus. "But what the hell does it *mean*!" Nick Blackburn demanded of Cotty Donaldson as they walked up the shallow exterior stone steps and stopped at the rear of the nave to gaze, stunned, at the gaping hole behind the altar and the morning sky brightly visible through it. "Who would break it? Who would, well, I don't know, bother? Why?"

They looked at each other and then a gleam came into Cotty's eyes. "There's that Hochschwender creep."

Nick blew out a mouthful of disgusted breath. "Do you think he would go this far?"

"Well, who else would?"

The students were filtering into their places in the Chapel, not at all with the usual virile briskness of the average morning, but silently, subdued, and inclined to glance most apprehensively around them. The faculty, coming into their places in the west transept, seemed to wrap themselves in a special, silent dignity, as though assisting at a funeral.

Wexford, long red and gray woolen scarf wrapped flamboyantly around his neck, appeared at the entrance of the Chapel, and stopped beside Nick.

"Somebody came to my room and told me about this," he said in a cold voice. "I didn't believe him. Who would have? Now I see it. I still don't believe it. Have I gone mad, or who has, or what?"

A walloping thought suddenly shook Nick Blackburn. "I uh," he began, "my uh brother Tug . . ."

Wexford turned to look at him. "What about Tug?"

"He's in the Infirmary. Concussion."

"So I heard. I'm sorry to hear it," replied Wexford in a why-bring-up-this-irrelevance-now voice.

"He's . . ." Struggling emotions contorted Nick's face. "He's off his nut. He might do anything. Not know it."

Wexford gazed at him. Then he said very calmly, "I don't believe it. He isn't capable of it. Even if he's in a daze or a trance or something. He would never do something so out of character. I don't believe it."

"Well, that's wonderful," burst out Nick, grinning and flushing. "That sure is white of you. But"—his hands began to twist the notebook they held as another thought smacked him—"he's um on the Devon Council. He uh has keys to the Chapel."

Wexford was suddenly suffused with energy. "It's all ridiculous and Tug Blackburn simply couldn't and wouldn't do it. We have to look somewhere else."

The bell summoning the school to Chapel was sounding its final tolls and they hurried to their places.

The service began with a stern hymn, "God of Our Fathers." Then the Headmaster, solemn in a gray tweed suit, moved to the lectern and began in an uncharacteristically low voice to speak of "vandalism."

Pete Hallam sat at his place in the front row of the transept, and as Dr. Wherry began to become angry, seemingly from the meaning of his own words, the sound of his own voice, and as an April wind whipped several of last fall's dead leaves through the grotesque hole where the window had been, and when a bird lighted momentarily on the window's frame, Pete felt an hallucinatory return, as though this were one of the innumerable bombed-out churches of Italy, as though war's chaos had ground its way to the edge of town, New Hampshire merging with Salerno, Devon blurring into the trapped horror of Anzio, this little Chapel a second Monte Cassino, nothing separate or safe, everything merging into a dangerously unpredictable miasma of risk and destruction. He grinned wryly to himself. They'd put me in the Psycho Ward if they knew what I was thinking. But as he glanced almost involuntarily at the jagged and meaningless shards which were all that remained of the memorial, and the weird spectacle of blue sky looming behind the altar of the Devon Chapel, he was struck by an inescapable sense of *déjà vu*, a double vision of yesterday's ruin merging into today's rickety order, violence like a subterranean river sometimes gushing to the surface in a tidal wave of destruction, sometimes flowing silently below, sometimes sending one geyser in a brief spurt upward to break a stained-glass window and menace the peace of a school.

"We will investigate this disgusting and sacrilegious outrage here at the school," the Headmaster was saying, "and appropriate and severe punishment will be meted out. For the rest, I ask you all to offer a prayer for the mentally disturbed person who would attack our dignified and beautiful memorial to the sons of Devon who suffered for their country."

There was a prayer and a final hymn, "Dear Lord and Father of Mankind Forgive Our Foolish Ways." Then in an atmosphere of unreality not unmixed with a kind of elation brought on by the outrageousness and egregiousness of the act, the students and faculty went murmuring out of the Chapel.

The schedule of morning classes proceeded with an air of normality. Everyone went to lunch where the name of Tug Blackburn passed from table to table as the unwitting perpetrator of the deed. "Of all people, Tug, the pillar of the school" . . . "Yeah, but a concussion is a concussion" . . . "If you're off your head, you can't think" . . . "He never liked *art*" . . .

Coming out of the dining room Nick and Cotty were stopped by Pete Hallam. "Let's drop over to the Infirmary and see Tug," he suggested to them.

"Should we?" asked Nick swiftly. "Isn't that too—wouldn't that uh—"

"I think we ought to talk to him for a minute or two," said Pete evenly.

"He isn't responsible," said Nick argumentatively. "I don't even think he knows where he is yet."

"Come on."

Nick and Cotty fell in beside Pete. They strode across the Center Common, the shrubbery here preening with spring, a fresh sunshine brightening even the classroom buildings, and lending the whole campus an air of innocent energy. Newness sprang everywhere, new greenness, fresh growths, a clarion airiness which washed across the school with the promising sweep of renewal.

"I don't think he did it," said Cotty reflectively. "I just don't think he did, off his nut or not."

The others paced along silently.

At the Infirmary Nurse Quimby looked up from the desk in her cubicle and said, "Oh!" as though the sight of these three particular people at this particular moment was the most unexpected thing in the world. "Yes? May I help you?"

Pete sighed—it reminded him so much of all the petty chickenshit of the Army—and then said, "I was here this morning. To see Tug Blackburn. Remember?"

"Oh." She fell into pretty confusion. "Yes, of course."

Not enough to do, Pete reflected abstractly.

There was a silence and then he said flatly, "We want to go up and see him again."

"Oh well I don't know . . . the doctor . . . I . . . well, I *guess* it's all right. Dr. Stanpole should be back in a few minutes."

"We'll go up. Won't be long."

In his room Tug was sitting propped up by some pillows reading a copy of the Boston *Globe*. When they came in he lowered it and looked a little wearily from one to the other.

"I guess you guys heard what I did," he then said, looking from Nick to Cotty.

"I don't believe it," said Cotty. "You don't remember doing it, do you?"

"Naw. I can't remember half the time what yesterday was."

"I don't think you did it."

"Well if I didn't, who did? Who would?"

There was a rather impressive silence and then Cotty said in his direct way, "Hochschwender."

"Hochschwender?" echoed Tug querulously, screwing up his face. "I know he puts on a big act, big Prussian act, maybe you could call it a big Nazi act, but take some rocks or something and smash that window all to hell. I don't see it."

"*Kristallnacht*," murmured Pete almost to himself.

"Huh?"

"Well," he murmured unwillingly, "it's just . . . there's precedent . . . German history."

"I don't get you," said Tug. He folded the newspaper backward and forward. Then he drew a deep, weary breath. "See? Now I'm getting suspicion turned on *him*."

"What do you mean, *you* are?" asked Nick sharply. "You aren't doing anything except to assume things about yourself that you can't be sure of."

"Uh, I'm pretty sure," said Tug resignedly. "If you knew the . . . *outrageous* things that have been going on in my head! For a while there I thought the Devon School Infirmary was the local Funny Farm down home, and that I'd been there all my life. I thought that chair you're sitting in, Pete, was a mastiff guard dog and if I moved he'd tear my throat out."

Pete nodded, looking at him soberly.

There was a knock on the door and then Dr. Stanpole, a calm, benevolent-looking presence, came in. "Well, you've got company," he said with a smile. "I guess it's okay, for a few minutes. How're you feeling?"

Tug nodded his head self-encouragingly.

"A bit more rest and he'll be all right. I myself wouldn't have," he added, glancing at Pete, "*necessarily* encouraged him to go over the Lip, at the Headwall, at Tuckerman's Ravine!"

Pete gazed with his light blue eyes back into the doctor's spectacles. Then he said, "I let him make his own decision. He's one of our best skiers."

"Mm. Hard to know when these boys are ready to make their own decisions. They're just on that dividing edge. Well . . . I guess we have to give them the benefit of the doubt." He moved across the room to take Tug's pulse. "No, it's all right. Don't leave. Stay for a few minutes. Say. Wasn't that something about the Memorial Window! Who would do a thing like that?" Then after a silence he remarked, "Your pulse beat is up, Tug. Too much company?"

The silence in the room became so heavy that someone had to shatter it. The doctor looked from Tug to the others and back again. "What's going on around here? What's up?"

Another clumsy silence ensued and then Pete began, "Well, the thing is—"

Tug cut in: "I think I busted that window, Doc. Who else would? When I was out of my head, sometime late last night. It's easy to slip out of here."

The doctor gazed at length down at him. "Now you sound like you're really off your head. You did take your sleeping pill last night? The nurse stayed and watched you take it?"

Tug nodded.

"That pill, for a healthy uncomplicated young athlete like you who hasn't had three sleeping pills in his life, that pill sent you into never-never land for eight solid hours and you couldn't possibly have moved from that bed."

Tug looked at him, blinking. "I never thought of that," he then mumbled.

Pete gradually uncoiled himself from a tight sitting position. Nick broke into his brightest grin. Cotty nodded in self-satisfaction.

Tug was looking around at the others and at the

room in general, as though seeing it all in a new and pleasing perspective.

A few minutes later they left the Infirmary and walked at a more ruminating pace back across the campus. "So where does that leave us?" Nick asked at last.

There was a pause which extended into thoughtful silence. Pete veered off to keep an appointment in the Administration Building and as soon as he was out of earshot Cotty Donaldson pronounced one word: "Hochschwender."

In the Butt Room at Pembroke House that afternoon at five The Boys came together.

"So it wasn't Tug."

"I knew it couldn't've been."

"Of course not."

"He'd never do anything like that, out of his head or not out of his head."

"It's the same as hypnotized people. You can only make them do what they'd do anyway."

"I knew he could never do anything so stupid, so—well—evil, you might say."

After a few moments of thought Chet said, "I . . . guess . . . we . . . all . . . really do . . . know who . . . did it . . . now . . . don't we."

There was another silence.

"I don't like things like that happening around here, myself," Cotty said in a deliberate tone of voice.

•   •   •   •

Eric Hochschwender lifted his single scull from its rack in the little boathouse just above the dam and waterfall in the Devon River and put it into the water. He admired this sleek little craft, enjoyed his independence in it. The various rowing crews used the wide river below the dam, the Naguamsett, but Eric far preferred his single scull, which he could row himself, which required no cooperation with others, and he also preferred rowing it in the narrow, winding little Devon River above the dam because it was more difficult, unsuitable really for any boat bigger than a rowboat or canoe. Pulling swiftly upstream in it required great skill and precision and control, and he was satisfied that he possessed all three, although with all his skill he sometimes ran aground. This kind of sport suited him exactly: entirely individual, and performed on the most difficult and inappropriate body of water in the area, where there was no one to compete with him, no one to share the experience even, where the sight of his lean blond self sliding in swift solitariness through the water presented to those who happened to see him a striking enigma, a graceful contradiction, a symbol of incongruous skill, a separate and defiant athlete setting his own tests for himself, and passing them, for himself.

His slim figure sliding by on the frail and graceful hull acquired a challenging, icy significance, utterly egregious, a Thoreau listening to his own distant drummer, of all things a Prussian drummer.

In his blue tank top and white shorts Eric pulled the scull easily upstream, glancing swiftly over his shoulder from time to time to correct his course and stay midstream.

It was revelation of a spring day. The season was anticipating itself: the temperature seemed to have gone up to around seventy-five degrees, and the shrubbery and the great overhanging trees and a newly sown field were struggling to burst into fullest bloom now that nature, after the grueling punishments of a New England winter, was suddenly so inviting. Hochschwender rowed on, humming "Wien, Wien."

He tried to take these workouts on the river as often as he could in the spring and fall, adding them to his regular Gym classes. His doctor in Boston had

carefully scheduled gradual increases in their stren-
uousness. Rheumatic heart! What a disgusting con-
dition: a childhood disease leaving him with an
impaired heart, supposedly for the rest of his life.
But if he persisted in his regimen of building up his
strength slowly and surely year by year, why perhaps by the time he was say thirty he might have
overcome it completely. Many times before, totally
determined and dedicated patients had surmounted
infirmities said to be incurable.

He had to be strong.

He irritated the hell out of most people: he knew
that. Well, there *were* certain favorable things to be
said about Nazi Germany. Hitler had ended the
Depression and the unemployment there, hadn't he?
He'd built the superb system of *Autobahns*, the envy
of the world. He'd made it possible for his country
to lead the world in jet planes, rocketry. Eric had
always been fascinated by scientific and engineering
advances.

His father, whom he worshiped, had been strongly
pro-Nazi until even in their neighborhood in Wisconsin that had become very inadvisable. Then his
father had just gradually become silent on the subject as the sweep of the war carried the Germans to
victory after victory, and then even more silent as
they slid to this terrible defeat.

As for all the hatred of Hitler, tales of his persecu-
tion of the Jews and Gypsies and Poles and the
Catholic Church and the Protestant churches, of sexual deviants and just about anybody who didn't suit
him, well all that was just based on rumor. The
newsreels of the piled bodies in concentration camps?
Faked.

His father had fallen silent sometime in 1940, about
the time of the Battle of Britain and Winston Churchill and his "blood, sweat and tears" and "we shall
fight on" speeches which the radio stations had drilled

into the ears of the American people from Bangor, Maine, to San Diego, California. Propaganda.

But Eric himself had never fallen silent and he was not going to start now. They said this was a free country, didn't they? He'd test all that out; he would continue to be the acid test for that. They believed in free speech, did they? He'd give them free speech. They said democracy flourished from the clash of opinions? He'd give them a clash of opinions, he'd give them something to clash about. Here in this rural backwater, this Devon School, he had certainly shaken them up all right. What a collection of little everyday conformists they were, thinking they were so independent, such individualists. He was the only individual in the place, with the possible exception of Wexford.

Wexford and that corny Memorial Window of his— and now, smashed to bits! It was something like the Reichstag fire . . . a mysterious outrage . . . a half-crazed scapegoat. Eric felt almost dizzy as he recalled the sight of that gaping hole behind the altar, with the stupid spring sky smiling all blue and innocent down into the desecrated church.

He rowed on under the little arching bridge which connected the Playing Fields with the Fields Beyond and the Stadium. He could see it on his left, a gray-white bank of seats where the rah-rah students watched those dumb oxes, the varsity football team, play their monolithic game. Football, a sport for oxen. In Germany they played fast and furious and inventive and ingenious soccer. Except for the war he felt sure his father would have sent him to Germany to complete his education. There, he knew, the school would have had real rigor, truly dedicated scholarship. And they said Devon was the very best America had to offer. It was just not good enough. No physical punishment when you deserved it! No rigor!

He rowed on, pleasurably warming up, pulling

the oars firmly and smoothly through the still water, the hull skimming lightly and gracefully over the surface, all his movements delicately unified with the slender craft, fusing himself and scull into a single coordinated, balancing propulsion, slipping almost soundlessly over the smoky, deep-green surface between ponderous trees.

Rounding a bend in the little river he came abreast of two old Revolutionary War cannons which had been placed on a little point of land, aiming downriver. Laughable. He pulled on past them, past a tree with pegs in it leaning out a little over the stream. Here that legendary Devon athlete had been injured a couple of summers ago, and had later died. There were rumors that his roommate had really been responsible. Eric would not be a bit surprised if that was true.

Leaving the tree behind him he swept farther upstream, deeper into uninhabited forest.

The stream was gradually narrowing and there were shallow places this far upriver, so he decided to turn about and go back. He particularly enjoyed the counterstroking involved in this maneuver, so neat and precise, turning a hundred and eighty degrees while staying virtually in the same spot.

Completing the turn, he looked over his shoulder to set his course and noticed two canoes rounding the bend and heading very purposefully toward him. Another moment and he recognized two members of that grandstanding bunch of athletes from Pembroke House in each canoe. As they drew closer he called out mockingly, "Oh gee! The Red Indians in their canoes are after me!"

There was no answering gibe from them; they moved swiftly up alongside him, one canoe on each side, then stopped. One of them, Donaldson, said, "Pull over to the shore. We want to talk."

"I've got nothing to talk to you about," Eric

replied irritably. "Let go of my oars. What the hell do you think you're doing!"

"Pull over to the shore," said Cotty Donaldson, "we want to talk."

"Get your goddam hand—" he began, and then Cotty jerked his port oar and Eric was pulled suddenly from his precarious perch on the scull, splashing into the icy water. "Swim over to the shore," said Cotty.

"What the bloody hell do—you bunch—"

"Don't say anything more," advised R.T., grimacing down at him. "You'll just regret it. Swim over to the riverbank. Or am I going to slap your face with this canoe paddle?"

Blond hair plastered down over his forehead, Eric glared as ferociously as he could up at them. It was impossible to get back on the skull from the water, even if they would have let him. He swam toward the river's bank, yelling, "If you bang up my scull in any way I'll—"

"Look out for your skull, Hochschwender," advised R.T.

Eric understood the play on words and it sent an odd little shock, a sudden small electric alarm, up the back of his neck.

The two canoes were swiftly beached. Eric stood in the mud as the four Pembroke Boys—Cotty, R.T., Chet and Guy—came up to him. "What the hell do you want?" he demanded, prowlike head thrown back, fixing them with narrowed blue eyes.

"It's about the window, Hochschwender," Cotty Donaldson said evenly. "That window was dedicated to a lot of guys who fought the enemy, your friends the Krauts. Some of those guys died. Then you come along and smash the window."

Hochschwender made a face of total disgust. "Why would I bother with your stupid window?"

"Who knows why you do anything?" replied Cotty

in a swift monotone. "You're not denying you did it. You just start asking the kind of questions we don't like. Why did you do it?"

Eric Hochschwender's face suddenly flushed. "You goddam bunch of horse's asses! I don't have to explain anything to you! What do you mean dragging me off my scull! Who the hell—!"

"You're not just off your scull," said R.T., "you're off your head." He swung around to look at the others. "Why are we standing here talking to this creep? Let's get him in the river and get it out of him."

"If you bunch of"—Eric began in a voice of constricted frenzy—"thugs put one goddam hand on *me*—" the last word a sudden yell as he was jerked toward the water, hustled into it up to his shoulders. From behind his head a strong hand thrust his head underwater. Then he was dragged to the surface. "You broke the memorial to our guys who died."

"You violated the school Chapel."

"You think we're going to let you get away with that, you lousy Kraut! Admit you did it! *Why* did you do it!"

Jaw locked, Eric rasped, "Let go of me, you hoodlums!"

"*Why* did you break the window!"

It went on and on, ritually, like those messianic unison roars of "Heil Hitler!" at the monstrously glorious rallies in Nuremberg, on and on, voices in waves—"*Why did you do it!*" echoing in his head, like those percussive roars at the gross rallies of Hitlerism. "*Why*" . . . and "*why*" and "*Why!*"

"You and your *Chapel* and your *window*!" he rasped. "What do I care a *shit*! You rotten bastards!" Bluish white, eyes staring, he took several sudden gasps of air. Then he fainted.

• • •

Nick Blackburn had been assigned the task of keeping Rob Willis out of the way and occupied while the others went up the river and dealt with Hochschwender.

Nick went to the suite in Saltonstall Hall where Hochschwender and Willis lived, and found Willis at a desk in the front room, typing. Willis asked him to come in and sit down and what could he do for him?

He struck Nick Blackburn as being very unlike his roommate. He was also from the Midwest, but his demeanor was contrastingly placid, his attitude accommodating, his voice quiet. He had brownish blond hair, grayish green eyes, small bones, and an overall air of not wanting to cause, be involved in, witness, or even hear about unpleasant scenes.

"Is it okay if I wait here for Eric?" Nick asked. He had never called or even thought of Hochschwender by his first name before. "I need some information about our American History assignment."

"Yeah, sure." Rob Willis returned tentatively to his typing.

"Nice room you've got here," observed Nick. It was in fact stark to the point of being penal, no school pennants, no leggy pinups, no family pictures. At least there were no Nazi flags or photos of Der Führer.

"It's nice to be a senior," said Rob quietly. "We get the best rooms, don't we?"

"Mm. Boy, wasn't that something at Chapel! That broken window. Gee-zooey."

Rob pivoted in his chair to look, blinking a little, across at him. "I was really shocked," he said in a sincere tone. "I just couldn't believe it."

"Who could?" Nick, sitting across the room at Hochschwender's desk, leaned forward, elbows on knees, hands clasped. "You know for a while there people thought my *brother* did it!"

"I know. I heard about it." Rob gazed at him inquiringly. "And?"

"What do you mean, 'and'?"

Rob rubbed the side of his face and then said, "Well, I mean we wondered—well, did he?"

Nick looked at him fixedly. You goddam two-faced crook, he thought bitterly, you *accomplice*! You know goddam well he didn't do it. Aloud he said, jaw set, "Tug himself didn't know. He *might* have done any-thing, even something as . . . loony as that. He'd had a concussion and was out of his head." Rob nodded placatingly at this. "And being out of his head and everything, maybe he was capable of that. But Doc Stanpole explained that he'd been knocked out with sleeping pills and couldn't have gotten out of his bed."

Rob grinned. "I'll bet you were sure glad to hear that."

I kind of like this little twerp, Nick thought unwill-ingly. How'd he ever get taken over by Hoch-schwender?

"Yeah well of course I was, even though I knew Tug, nutty as a fruitcake or not, couldn't do any-thing *that* loony. He just couldn't. Now we have the proof." Nick had been looking down at his hands. Now he looked across at the guileless grayish-green eyes of Rob Willis. "So the question is: who did?"

Rob shook his head in confusion. "Search me."

What could I find? Nick asked himself. The "weap-on," they think, was the long pole with the hook on it used to open the high-up Chapel windows. It was found lying on the floor by the altar. No fingerprints.

Nick decided the time had come to stop this cha-rade. By now Hochschwender was doubtless getting the Second if not the Third Degree somewhere up the Devon River. It was time for Nick to get corrobo-ration for the confession.

"Look um Rob, there's no point in beating around

the bush. We all know who did it. *You* of all people know who did it. The question is," Nick added, his voice acquiring an almost confidential tone, "did you go along and help Hochschwender do it?" Leaning elbows on knees, Nick contemplated the smallish figure across the room.

Rob Willis went into a kind of momentary nervous seizure. His body snapped into recoil, tense and vibrating. He was transformed before Nick's eyes: suddenly the comradely link between him and Hochschwender was nakedly displayed. "You—what are you talking about! Eric didn't bust that window! Now you're nutty as a fruitcake, not your brother. He wouldn't do that. He wouldn't even be bothered doing that! You don't even know him. None of you guys know him. He's got—you don't know how much—he's got nothing but contempt for you guys and your Chapel and your window! You think he'd bother going out at night and break that thing, risk getting expelled, risk his future career! For that stupid window? You don't even know what you're talking about. You guys—you think you're so important, the big stars, rich families—you guys think you are everything and so you think you know everything. I'll tell you: you don't know Eric, and you sure as hell don't know me if you think I'd go along with anything so crazy. You guys"—the corners of his mouth came down scornfully—"are just too full of yourselves, throwing your weight around and thinking you're God Almighty. You don't own this school and I don't care how much your father contributes." His eyes darted excitedly around the room, his fists were clenched, he seemed to want to throw something at Nick Blackburn. "You're plain nuts, brother, if you think Eric would mess around with your stupid Chapel and your stupid window! He wouldn't give you guys the satisfaction. He's—he's . . . I'll tell you what he is. He's *proud*!"

Nick found he had been holding his breath through most of this. His stomach muscles were taut, as though braced for a blow to the solar plexus. His eyes followed every gesture, ears every inflection. He sat immobilized, trying to reason, to think, to decide, to act. God. Good holy God. Nick felt himself sliding sickeningly to the conclusion that Eric Hochschwender, top student Nazi or not, had had nothing to do with the shattering of the Memorial Window.

●　　●　　●

The moment a death-pale Hochschwender slumped into their arms, the Pembroke Boys instantly and in unison shifted to an entirely different set of reactions, a much more congenital one to them. They suddenly were being called on to aid someone in trouble.

Swiftly lifting him into a canoe, they wrapped Eric in what pieces of clothing there were at hand to keep him warm, and with Cotty in the stern and R.T. in the bow they began paddling swiftly back down the river. Guy and Chet followed, one in the canoe, one awkwardly rowing the single scull.

Eric regained consciousness several times, but then lapsed back. The canoe shot past the cannons and was beached at the foot of the Playing Fields.

With Cotty under one shoulder and R.T. under the other, they hustled him at a fast trot across the fields. Never had they seemed so vast, so needlessly spacious, so wastefully extensive. At last, panting and exhausted, they came up to the Gym, commandeered a car and sped Eric, now dimly conscious, his face occasionally suffused and rosy, then draining to a deathly pallor, toward the Infirmary. The physical closeness as he lolled between them in the front seat, the urgency of their mission, the intertwined necessities of the emergency, the shared fright, all fused The Boys and the Kraut into an intimacy which befuddled everyone.

Cotty hurtled the car up the gravel Infirmary driveway and skidded to a stop. R.T. ran inside and Cotty began lifting Eric out of the car. We're always bringing someone to the *Infirmary*, Cotty growled desperately to himself.

· · ·

Nick Blackburn was still seated at Hochschwender's desk, struggling with the remnants of his confrontation with Rob Willis. He was saying, "Well we didn't necessarily think Eric did it, but with those letters last fall to *The Devonian* and all, we naturally—" when the door slammed open and a student said breathlessly, "Hochschwender's in the Infirmary. Something happened to him on the river." The rest of the words Nick was about to say stayed in his throat.

Rob hurled a glance of terminal loathing at Nick Blackburn and then stalked out of the room. After a stunned minute, Nick followed.

At the Infirmary Eric had been quickly installed in a room across the hall, as it happened, from Tug Blackburn's.

The Pembroke Boys—Cotty and R.T. and Chet and Guy—drifted disconsolately around the waiting room on the ground floor. Nobody found anything worth saying. The main door of the Infirmary suddenly swung open and Rob Willis came in. He looked at them with a wide-eyed stare of amazed indictment. They couldn't look back at him. "Where is he?" Rob demanded in a flat and menacing voice.

"He's—" Cotty began uncertainly, "in a room upstairs. He—we found him up the river. He all of a sudden I guess fainted."

Rob stared at him with his widened, greenish eyes. "What'd you do to him?" he demanded in this level, menacing voice.

"Do to him? What do you mean, do to him?"

"Don't make up some story to me, Captain Blood. Blackburn was just in my room. You—all—you bums—you think Eric broke that window in the Chapel. What'd you do to him? Did he have a heart attack?"

"A *heart* attack!" said Cotty in an aghast voice.

"He's got a rheumatic heart," muttered Rob in a tone of contemptuous boredom. "You don't bother to know about that. Did he have an attack?"

"I—no, that wasn't any *heart* attack. He just kind of swooned. Too much exertion. Rowing."

Mrs. Quimby came at a fast trot out from behind her cubicle and scurried up the stairs. There was a general commotion audible above, Dr. Stanpole's voice calling for something, the sound of a wheeled cart being rushed down the hallway, then complete silence.

In the waiting room the students sat or stood and stared. Rob Willis sat down on a bench and looked straight in front of him.

Nick Blackburn came slowly through the front door. Something in the atmosphere of the waiting room made him stop there and lean against the wall next to the door.

After a protracted period Dr. Stanpole, followed by Mrs. Quimby, came down the stairs. He was nodding abstractly to himself. Then he said in a low, tired voice, "His heart wasn't strong enough. We couldn't quite make it. Tried. Just couldn't quite make it." He let out a long breath. "How sudden death can be, a light going out."

There was a long, stunned silence and then Rob Willis, speaking as though not addressing anybody, as though going into a soliloquy, said in a voice which was at first small and constricted, "You've got a bunch of murderers here. These guys are a bunch of killers. They're hanging around here, and a half-hour ago they put my friend Eric to death on the river. You've got a gang of killers standing around the waiting room here. Is anybody going to do anything about it? Or is that the way things go? They kill another student and nobody does anything?" His voice was by now wobbling out of control.

Mrs. Quimby, who had gone to her cubicle, came back. "The Headmaster and Mr. Hallam are on their way," she told the doctor.

"Good," he sighed with heartfelt relief: "I just lost a student in a room upstairs," he muttered, more or less to himself. "Now, downstairs, someone is accusing someone of murder." He pronounced this last word in a deep, sorrowing, fatigued way, the ultimate letdown word, the antithetical word to "doctor" and "medicine" and "cure."

Dr. Stanpole went into his office next to the cubicle and began telephoning. None of the students said anything. They remained where they were.

• • •

Tug Blackburn had been having a nap. Dimly in his half-sleep he heard some of the commotion across the hallway, the sudden rushing confusion, the unearthly stillness, then the slow footsteps going downstairs.

Fully awake now, he wondered what it had been about. Sliding out of bed, moving with the instinctive furtiveness of a hospital patient not sure if he is violating some regulation, he crept across the corridor and peered in around the ajar door of the room.

Someone was lying motionless in the bed. There was a tank of oxygen beside the bed. There was no sound in the room, not even of breathing. Some shock of alarm began to clamp itself on Tug's mind. Who was that in the bed? He crept into the room, then he recognized the chiseled features of Eric Hochschwender beneath the taut waxen skin of the face.

It was obvious that he was dead but it was not possible that he was dead. It was so out of synchronization with everyday expectations that Tug could not accept it, take it in. He moved softly back into the hallway and across into his own room. He got into bed.

I must still be hallucinating, he thought. I must have had a concussion and a half.

•　•　•

After a while a car could be heard coming up the driveway and stopping. In a few moments the Headmaster and Pete Hallam came into the Infirmary waiting room. They nodded to the group, and the Headmaster then joined Dr. Stanpole in his office. A few minutes later the two of them came out and went upstairs. Then they came down again.

"I want all you boys to come with me to the Headmaster's house," Dr. Wherry said unemphatically. "You'll come too, Pete." They all trailed in a subdued, dutiful line out to the cars and drove to the big old white house.

Dr. Wherry led them through a dark reception hall into a big and rather shabby den-library, old books lining almost all the wall space, heavy overstuffed armchairs, two elderly sofas, an indeterminate-colored, worn rug, tables piled with books, an unplayed-looking baby grand piano, dried flowers in vases, gloomy reproductions of Piranesi engravings, the whole room shadowed, in half-light.

The four students from Pembroke House and Nick Blackburn sat down on one of the sofas, its arms, and the floor in front of it. Rob Willis sat alone on the other sofa. Across from them the Headmaster and Pete Hallam took armchairs.

"Now tell me what happened," said Dr. Wherry evenly.

Cotty Donaldson said, "Well, we went up the

river, took two canoes just to go up the river, the four of us, Nick Blackburn wasn't with us."

"No," cut in Rob Willis, "he came to my room, Eric's and my room. He came to accuse us—"

"Wait a minute," said Pete. "One at a time—don't you think, Dr. Wherry?"

"Yes. The four of you just wanted to paddle up the river, is that it?"

"That's all," put in R.T. hurriedly.

The Headmaster then asked, "Where did you come upon—first see Eric Hochschwender?"

"Pretty far up the river," answered Cotty.

"And how was he, what was he doing?"

"Slumped in his scull," said Cotty.

"Rowing," said R.T. at the same time.

There was a stiff stillness and then the headmaster, looking slowly from one to the other, said dryly, "Well, which was it, was he 'rowing' or was he 'slumped'?"

"Well he was—" began Cotty.

"I saw him first," blurted R.T. "Prob'ly nobody saw him rowing but me. He was, see, rowing, and then he slumped."

"What did you see, Hanley?"

Guy Hanley, man of few words, mumbled, "I was sort of looking at the bottom of the inside of the canoe. I was paddling stern, I uh guess I just didn't look up."

"Eventually I presume that you did look up." There was a tight pause until Guy nodded unwillingly in response.

"And then what did you see?"

After another pause Guy muttered, "Hochschwender and the scull."

"He was still in the scull?"

Another pained pause and then Guy murmured, "Yes, sir."

"Was he moving?"

"I—uh—I think . . ." Guy's face began to work.

"The thing is," put in Cotty, "we were all pretty shocked and it's hard to remember."

The Headmaster said, "I would tend to doubt that you can't remember."

Cotty's eyes widened for a moment. He stared, at a loss.

Dr. Wherry's usually imperturbable face momentarily acquired a desperate look, almost a hunted look. Turning to Pete, he said, "Mr. Hallam, you're the faculty adviser to these boys in Pembroke House. Can you unravel any of this?"

Pete had been coaching at the Gym and was in gray warm-up togs. He said, "We're going to have to get a complete picture of what happened, what everyone saw and did. No one is accusing anyone of anything. You—"

Rob Willis said in an undertone, "They did it. Everybody knows."

Pete paused, looked at him, and then said, "We'll have your view of this later. You weren't there on the river, were you?"

"No," he said defiantly.

"Well then, you can't contribute anything on the question at hand: what was Hochschwender doing, how was he, when Cotty and the others first saw him? Since you're his roommate you can stay. Don't say anything."

"Sir," Rob began in an almost suave tone (How could I have thought I liked this little menace? Nick was thinking.), "Eric had rheumatic fever when he was eleven. It affected his heart. Is that relevant, by any chance?"

Pete looked at him fixedly. "Of course it is. Dr. Stanpole had that information."

"Well then," pursued Rob, still in his maddeningly condescending manner, "is the fact that Blackburn there and these other punks thought Eric broke that Chapel window, is *that* relevant, by any chance?"

"How do you know that?"

"Because"—Rob's voice was suddenly a harsh blare—"Blackburn came to our room and accused him of it, to me, while Eric was up on the river. *That* make any difference?"

Another taut silence closed over the dimly illuminated room.

"Get on with it," the Headmaster said in muffled desperation.

"What we have to know, first and foremost, is what state Eric was in when you first saw him on the river," said Pete.

"He was okay at first," Cotty said flatly. "We started talking to him and then he slumped over his oars. Then we brought him back to the Infirmary."

R.T., Chet and Guy nodded solemnly at these words, gazing open-eyed at the Headmaster.

Into Pete's mind to his chagrin sprang the college-boy song lyrics:

> *We are poor little lambs*
> *Who have lost our way,*
> *Baa, baa, baa,*
> *We are little black sheep*
> *Who have gone astray,*
> *Baa, baa, baa.*

Dr. Wherry sat motionless for a long time, then getting up he said very wearily, "You boys can go now. We'll continue this invest— this um thing later. The Dean will send for you." He walked with them to the front door of the house and then came back to Pete in the library. "Before I make that phone call that crucifies heads of schools," he said, "I'm going to have a drink. Scotch all right?"

Pete nodded.

When they had their drinks in hand, they sat down in the chairs again. "Of course they're lying," the Headmaster murmured despairingly.

Pete drew a breath. "Well, we're not getting the whole truth from them."

"The Dean will be back from Boston tomorrow. Out of town on a day like this! He will have to conduct any investigation. I think there may have to be a faculty committee to assist him. You will be on it. And where will it all end? With the police? *Manslaughter* charges?"

"Do you know why this happened?" Pete said suddenly. "Whatever *did* happen?"

The Headmaster looked at him.

"Because these boys are so goddam frustrated. They're eaten up with frustration, so eaten up they don't know which way to look."

"But why?"

"Because," said Pete with a helpless shrug, "they missed the war. They're riddled with guilt over that. Since they've been thirteen years old everything's been the war, the war. Suddenly, just when they're becoming old enough for it, it's over! They'll never get into it. Kids their age enlisted the day they turned seventeen and got killed on Iwo Jima. These boys know that. They're guilty! So somebody breaks their gesture to the older soldier boys, that damn window. What're they going to do? They're going to punish the guy who broke the window, good and proper, that's what they're going to do." He stared at the floor broodingly.

"But," intoned the Headmaster in his most lugubrious voice, "he wasn't punished, beaten up. He was—he's dead. And," he forced himself on, "I wonder if he really did destroy that window."

• • •

Wexford was in the basement of the Chapel building, playing the piano. "Clair de Lune" delicately rolled from the piano, followed by "The Blue Danube Waltz" and then "All the Things You Are" and "If I Loved You" and "Night and Day" and "Deep Purple" and "That Old Black Magic." Normally he didn't play his popular repertoire here in the practice room, sticking dutifully to the classics and the "semiclassics." But today even the latter seemed too rigorous for his free-flowing mind and spirit. He felt—and trying to put his feelings into words they suddenly coalesced into a song which he promptly played: "I Feel Like a Feather in the Breeze." That was it exactly.

Wexford concluded this popular recital to himself, got up and went upstairs. Peering into the Chapel, he saw that the gap left by his Memorial Window had been boarded over with raw, light brown panels of wood. They looked even more obscene than the gaping hole left by the shattered glass.

Coming out of the Chapel, he turned left and headed toward the Administration Building, where the Headmaster wanted to see him. As he walked down the lane Tug Blackburn came out of the Infirmary, carrying a small satchel. They met at the bottom of the Infirmary driveway.

"So they're letting you out," observed Wexford roguishly. "You're back in your right mind, I take it?"

"I guess so. If anything could have driven me around the bend permanently, it was walking across the hall in there and seeing a dead body in the room, and then realizing it was Hochschwender." He emitted a blast of exasperated breath. "Some guys carried him in and the doctor put him to bed and then he sort of just died."

"Oh? Rumor has it that it was your buddies from Pembroke House who brought him in."

"Is that right?" Tug looked surprised. "That's funny. They don't hang around with Hochschwender."

"I'll say they don't."

"Where'd they run into him?"

"On the river," answered Wexford dryly. "I gather they went to talk to him about the Memorial Window, alone, up there."

"They went to talk to him up the river?"

"Yes."

"That's very peculiar."

"Isn't it."

"Oh. Listen," Tug said. "I almost forgot. They want the keys back, the Dean's office does, all the keys to the Chapel. Got yours on you?"

Wexford recoiled, then glared at him. "I don't have any key to the Chapel. You're crazy."

"Sure you do. Remember? I gave you one last September, so you could practice when it was locked."

"You're completely wrong, Blackburn. Concussion. That can be more serious than people thought, apparently. Your memory got jumbled. I never had any key to the Chapel."

"But"—Tug screwed up his face in puzzlement—"didn't you come over to my room in Pembroke House and get one? Sure you did. I remember."

"No, Blackburn. You must have really hit your head very hard indeed on Mount Washington." He began to move on. "Maybe you need shock treatment," he tossed over his shoulder.

I don't know, grumbled Tug to himself. I think I'm already getting shock treatments, one after another.

• • •

The Headmaster's office in the Jeremiah Jones Administration Building was just as cheerful as his library at home was gloomy: large-paned, gleaming windows, high ceiling, light graceful furniture, neo-Georgian airiness and balance.

Dr. Wherry himself, in a light tan suit, looked ill. "Sit down, Wexford." There was a silence in the bright sunny room. Wexford waited, looking across the large, neat desk at the Headmaster with a patient, expectant expression on his face. Between his legs his long-fingered, not-quite-clean hands worked each other with suppressed convulsiveness.

"You will of course," the Headmaster began with an effort, "have to report the incidents—the very sad, very regrettable, the shocking incidents of these past days in the next issue of *The Devonian*, of course. Now. You know I and the faculty want to give the paper maximum freedom, maximum latitude, minimum of control, supervision. You know that. We never censor anything. But. We do advise and we do in the end have the last word, certainly when it comes to anything as tragic as this."

"I quite understand," said Wexford pleasantly.

"I want simply—and *briefly*—to report what happened, and *nothing more*. Is that clear?"

"Perfectly, sir."

The Headmaster cast an uncharacteristically cold and shrewd glance across the desk at him. "Now, tell me what you are going to report. What did happen?"

"Why," he drawled easily, "a person or persons unknown came to the Chapel in the middle of last Sunday night and shattered the Memorial Window. The other story is—"

"That's really too brief an account," put in the Headmaster. "Too many people know other facts, and however unpleasant, baffling . . . ignominious they are, they will have to be reported. From which side was the window broken?"

"Well"—Wexford leaned forward in his chair, speaking in a confiding tone—"from the inside, I understand."

"Yes," said Dr. Wherry wearily. "However bizarre that may sound. And the object used?"

"The window pole?"

"Correct."

"Should I include anything else?"

"I don't think so," replied the Headmaster. He sighed. "If between now and publication you come upon any additional information, anything at all, you will come to me first, before printing it."

"Certainly, sir."

"Now"—Dr. Wherry suddenly looked as though he hadn't slept for a week—"the other tragic story."

"Yes, well, as I understand it, Hochschwender, Eric Hochschwender went rowing in his single scull on the river and overexerted himself and had a heart attack. He had an injured heart from a boyhood case of rheumatic fever. Other students found him and brought him—"

"*Rushed* him."

"*Rushed* him," repeated Wexford with the faintest of smiles, "to the Infirmary. Despite all the efforts of the professional staff there, they were unable to save him. Funeral arrangements," he added, a twinkle somewhere at the back of his eyes, "are incomplete. Shall I say to omit flowers?"

Dr. Wherry gazed for a long time across the desk at him. Then he said in an odd, fundamental tone of voice, "Mr. Wexford, is it possible that you are in some way making light of all this?"

"Oh of course not, sir."

Another long gaze, Headmaster to student, and then Dr. Wherry said, "I believe that will be all, Mr. Wexford." He never took his eyes from the lean figure of Wexford as he sauntered from the room. The Headmaster had never addressed a student as "Mr." before. Something about Wexford, his ambiguous strength, or his simulated adulthood, or his moral dubiousness, had made him do so now. With his right hand Dr. Wherry began to rub his face up and down, up and down.

•   •   •   •

Rob Willis, having been sent for, came to Pete Hallam's quarters in Pembroke House. It was five o'clock on the afternoon following Hochschwender's death.

Pete motioned him to a chair in his sparsely furnished old sitting room–study.

"Do you want me to ask you questions, or is there just something you want to tell me?"

"I don't need any questions," replied Rob, staring at him. "There's something, two things, I'd like to say."

"Go ahead."

"Blackburn, the other one, not the one who lives here in Pembroke House, came to see me yesterday while they were . . . while those other guys were—you know what they were doing."

Pete looked expressionlessly back at him.

"And," Rob went on in a flat, harsh voice, "Blackburn accused Eric of breaking that window and thought maybe I was an accomplice."

Pete looked fixedly at him. "Did he break it?"

"Of *course* not. He never left our room that night. I sleep—I sleep like a moth. If he turns over in the other bed, I wake up. He couldn't have left our room without my hearing it, waking up. Besides. Eric would never do anything so stupid in a thousand years. Eric is *intelligent.*" He stopped, laughed harshly. "I mean, Eric *was* intelligent. How's that for sickening? Dead. Seventeen years old."

Pete nodded soberly. "It's a damn shame. And you're right, Eric had a very high intelligence quotient."

"He was much too smart to do anything that stupid. Nobody understands—understood him. He didn't want to have anything to do with the schoolboy baloney around here, that's what he called it. He wanted to do as well as possible scholastically

and go to MIT. He thought that window was baloney. He thought the Pembroke Boys were baloney.
He never broke that window. And they killed him."

Oh my back oh Lord God oh Jesus, Pete repeated
inwardly. I think maybe he's telling the truth. Not
that burning down the Chapel would have justified
abusing the kid the way they must have done.

Going out of Pete's front door Rob Willis encountered Cotty Donaldson and R.T. on the walk. "Murderers," he muttered harshly in their faces, and
walked on. Pete, standing in the doorway, heard it.
As they passed him, Cotty and R.T. looked first at
Rob, then at Pete with quick, stricken glances.

Oh Christ, Pete groaned to himself. That monster
war—sending last thin death waves still reverberat-
ing around the world, even here to this little rural
corner.

•   •   •

Rob Willis went to see Wexford in his tiny *Devonian*
office. Wexford took him for a walk. "Out here no
one can hear us," he explained. "Anywhere else,
my office, your room, anywhere inside, you never
know. Well?"

"Put it in the paper," said Rob. "They killed him,
the Pembroke guys."

"Proof?"

Rob described Nick Blackburn's visit to him.

"That's certainly very suggestive," observed Wexford. "It would indicate that they were 'after' Eric, as
we used to say in grammar school. I wonder exactly
what did happen up the river."

"We'll never know, that's it," said Rob bitterly.
"This whole thing will just peter out. No witnesses."

"Oh yes, there was a witness, aside from the
Pembroke Boys."

"There was? Who?"

"Eric Hochschwender."

"Yes," Rob replied scornfully, "but Eric's—"

"Did he come to, say anything to Dr. Stanpole?"

Rob stopped in his tracks. "I don't know," he said wonderingly.

Wexford turned briskly back toward his office. "I'm a journalist, am I right? I'm *it* around here."

•   •   •

Dr. Stanpole received Wexford in his office in the Infirmary.

"Two students dying on me in just a couple of years. And for the seventeen preceding years that I've been at Devon, not one, not coming even remotely close. Do you know what it is? I'll tell you what it is. Pete Hallam explained it to me, and he's right. It's that infernal war. It sends out death rays. It's not satisfied with the millions of soldiers blown to pieces on the battlefields, with all the sailors drowned, or all the pilots incinerated in their planes, the civilians blasted to pieces in their homes. No. That's not enough. It sends out death rays to little peaceful corners of the world like this, and picks somebody off. Then it sends out another death ray, and picks somebody else off."

Has our good doctor been drinking? Wexford wondered coolly, gazing analytically at him. No, I guess not. But he certainly is unstrung.

"Dr. Stanpole," Wexford said in his rather elegant, peremptory manner, "in doing my story for the paper on this death, Eric Hochschwender's, so sad, very regrettable, I know how you feel . . . death rays . . . hmm, I didn't know Mr. Hallam thought in concepts like that." Wexford had begun ruminating aloud to himself. "More to him than I supposed, perhaps." Then looking back again at the doctor in a slightly rattled way. "What I'm saying is, or rather asking, is one thing."

Dr. Stanpole gazed at him with a mixture of tiredness and doggedness. "Yes?"

"Did Eric regain consciousness at all after they brought him in here?"

"I think you might say he was semiconscious for a few very brief intervals."

Wexford's hazel eyes flared. "Did he *say* anything?"

The doctor's gaze remained fixed on him. "What kind of thing?"

"Anything. Anything at all. Especially anything about what happened on the river."

"I don't think," he answered, removing his glasses to pinch the bridge of his nose, "that's something to put in the paper, if he did."

"Dr. Stanpole," replied Wexford, more peremptorily than ever, "the paper, the press, that's the place to put rumors to rest. I ought to tell you that the school is rife with rumors, of, well, Hochschwender being abused by those students up the river, and that that's what brought on the heart attack."

There was a long pause and then Dr. Stanpole said slowly and reluctantly, "There were only a few words I could catch. He repeated the word 'why' several times. I thought he seemed to be saying, 'They said why and why and why.' That's really all, and it could mean anything or nothing."

"Thank you very much, Dr. Stanpole," said Wexford, rising.

In the lobby downstairs Mrs. Quimby beckoned him into her cubicle. "Oh Mrs. *Quimby*," Wexford said very cordially indeed, "*just* the person I want to talk to. Of *course*. May we have a talk?"

"Why certainly. You were talking to the doctor about the circumstances of Eric Hochschwender's passing?"

"You bet I was."

"Well . . ."

"Yes?"

As she spoke her eyes roved continually back and forth, as though she were a lifeguard at the beach

scanning her field of vision for drowning swimmers.
"I was alone with him after I ran upstairs for a few
moments, just a few seconds really, and I said, 'What
happened? What brought this on?' and do you know
what he said to me?"

Wexford's eyes gleamed into hers.

"He said," she went on avidly, " 'They drowned
me.' "

Wexford settled back on his heels, restraining himself from kissing her. "And what are you going to
do with this information?" he inquired in his stead-
fast voice.

"Why nothing," she replied in an almost shocked
tone. "I'm not going to involve myself in any way
in this. With, you know, the Dean and, God forbid,
I don't know—the *police*! Not at all. But I thought I
just might *mention* it to you because I—it's too much
for me to just sit on all by myself. I'm afraid to
tell Dr. Stanpole or anybody on the faculty. They
might, I don't know, *force* me to get involved. And I
won't, I just won't. It's too *amorphous*. That's what it
is. Too amorphous. But you are the editor of the
paper and you have your channels and you have
your sources. Pretend"—she looked at him almost
mischievously—"that this was an anonymous phone
call. Treat it like that."

"I will, Mrs. Quimby," he replied with smiling
vigor. "That I will, Mrs. Quimby."

• • •

"Just checking," said Wexford, sinking into a battered chair in the Pembroke House Butt Room. "Tying
any loose ends to my story. About Eric's death."

Eric's death, repeated Nick inwardly. Nobody but
Willis ever called him Eric. Wexford is sure being
polite to him, now that he's dead.

"Loose ends," blurted Chet. "There aren't any."

Wexford's eyes slid in his direction and then he

said, "Was he rowing or was he passed out when you got to him? There seems to be much confusion about that."

"He was both!" Guy suddenly snarled.

"Both?" Wexford's eyebrows went up and down mockingly. "That isn't even funny. Your story, or rather your stories, are becoming more and more confused, boys."

"Just what," said Cotty bluntly, leaning forward to stare across the shabby room at him, "are you driving at?"

Wexford paused for several moments for the tension in the room to mount. It was rather like playing the piano. Dramatic pause. Down on the pedal. *Accelerando!*

"You see," he began in his most confident and confiding tone, "Eric was able to say something about what happened to him with you boys, after he got to the Infirmary."

The silence which followed these words pierced his eardrums: truly it seemed to deafen. Wexford felt an overwhelming sense of triumph surge up in him. Now he knew the truth: guilty.

And what would he do with his certainty? A sense of power so inebriating that he thought it must be visible suffused him. Lowering his eyes, he then said, "I guess you know what he—"

"Wexford," cut in Cotty, "you make any insinuations in the paper about anything that happened on the river and we'll sue you for every Wexford nickel there is."

"Oh," responded Wexford, grinning and playfully fiddling with a pen in his hand, "I wouldn't dream of printing anything. It's just"—he paused, as though searching for the right form of expression—"that I"—he looked up at Cotty, then at the others—"think you should know that I know. That's all."

There was heavy breathing in the room. There was a sense that something was about to explode.

"Well," Wexford said cordially, getting up, "good-bye." Then a twinkle came into his eyes. "You know the etymology of that word, don't you? Etymology, Hanley, means 'source.' 'Good-bye' is a corruption of 'God be with you.' Corruption, corruption," he finished gaily, striding out of the room.

When there was no one left in the room except The Boys, Cotty said in a kind of muttered groan, "How could we have done it?"

"We never meant to," Guy put in, struggling with himself.

"Yes, but we did it," said Cotty.

"We never knew about the heart," said Chet: "the," not "his," heart; the impersonality made it slightly more tolerable.

"We did it," concluded Cotty, "and we'll have to live with it, and that means there's something criminal about us."

• • •

Of course they're capable of violence, Wexford warned himself as he walked rapidly along a campus cross-walk toward his dormitory.

The perfumes of May hung in the air. The great overarching trees were filling out with summer leaves. The variegated buildings, the formal court-yards and wide-ranging fields of the fine old academy were settling toward summer's somnolence.

But instinctively he heard an answering voice inside him say that he was safe, completely safe. Something happened on the river—but how would he ever know exactly? Hochschwender had assuredly not died of drowning. He was sure that The Boys had been themselves seized by some sudden rage, a rush of violence which had carried them far past where they had meant to go.

And now they were in a total and shocked reaction to that. Their own capacity for brutality had stunned them. The last thing they would do now would be to attack anybody, even himself, even though he knew the truth.

• • •

Pete Hallam told Wexford to come to his rooms in Pembroke House at nine that night.

"Well, here we are again," observed Wexford brightly, sailing in. "The seasons come, the seasons go, as they sing at Yale. The last time I was here I was wrapped up like an Eskimo. Goodness, that rhymes—go, Eskimo—and now a polo shirt and slacks will do. New England. What variations! Like Bach. What a climate!"

"Sit down," said Pete, going himself to sit at his desk and face Wexford, who took a chair beside the cold fireplace. "Wexford, what do you think you know about what happened with Hochschwender on the river? Other than what's generally known?"

"Well," answered Wexford in a voice deep in his throat, half-surprised, half-welcoming, "that's a very direct question, isn't it?"

"What's your answer to that question?"

"Why"—he rolled his eyes around the sparse room—"your little gang here in Pembroke House, if it's being direct that you want, your little gang, four of them, jumped Hochschwender up the river. They jumped him, they beat him up and—"

"There were no bruises," said Pete in a mechanical voice, "on Eric Hochschwender."

"Well, you see, people don't bruise when they're tortured the way your Boys tortured Hochschwender. They practically drowned him."

Wexford was beginning to savor the unearthly silences he could induce by stating these things to these people. The sense of power flowed through him again.

Finally Pete Hallam said, "I'm sure there's no proof, or even evidence, of that at all."

"No real courtroom proof, if that's what you mean, sir. Your pet students are safe."

"Just a minute."

"They're completely safe. I can't testify against them," he pressed on, speaking emphatically, frowning across the room at Pete, "and the person who can, won't. They're certainly guilty of manslaughter, and they're going to get off scot-free. The Devon Council! Well, if those are the highest ideals of Devon . . ."

Pete stared at him for a full minute. Wexford remained seated, legs crossed, left foot casually swinging up and down.

Then Pete got up, went to the door, walked down the hall and soon returned. He was followed into the room by Tug Blackburn. Pete closed and locked the door and returned to his chair by the desk. Tug sat in the chair across from Wexford's in front of the fireplace.

"I understand you denied you had a key to the Chapel to Tug here," said Pete in a flat voice.

Wexford sat up. "Key to the Chapel? What's that got to do with anything? How do I know? *Cna*-pull, Lordee me, who cares about that?"

"Do you say you did not get a key to it last fall from Tug?"

"Of course I do, why, last fall, eight months ago, I don't know. Why should I? Of course not. Who cares?"

Tug opened a notebook he had been carrying. He got up and crossing in front of the fireplace pointed to a line on a page. "This is your signature. That's where you signed for the key."

An intake of breath and then Wexford blurted, "Well, so what? And that signature there shows that

Elliott Parker had a key, and *that* shows that Morton Gagstatter had a key, and—"

"Those keys," cut in Pete, "were returned, a little while ago, before the Memorial Window got broken. The Dean decided not to have those keys floating around the campus. Tug collected them all. He just overlooked yours until now."

"But he *didn't!*" burst out Wexford, smiling and flushed. "He came and got mine just last week. His concussion, he forgot."

There was another shimmering silence and then Pete said almost gently, "But you said to him yesterday and to me just now that you never had a key."

Wexford was staring straight in front of him, flushed, his mouth forming its curious *O* shape, like an old man's, like the mouth of someone seeking to form a word in an unknown language, like a hungry infant's.

"And so," continued Pete in his most level tone, "you went into the Chapel and shattered the window you'd put there. And of course you knew Eric Hochschwender would be suspected of it. And of course you knew the Pembroke House group were very likely to take matters into their own hands."

The flush had drained from Wexford's face. He bit his lip cogitatively. Then the beginnings of a smile worked at the curves of his mouth. "Sir," he said in his cultivated, confident voice, "I believe that's what is called in legal circles 'pure speculation.' And who would believe it? It just doesn't make any sense. Me break my own Memorial Window?" He got up. "Will you excuse me if I go now? Final exams, you know. Even *I* have to study now." Reaching the door he turned, and thrust his hand into his pocket. "Oh yes. Here," and he tossed the key to the Chapel on the table.

After making sure that Wexford was definitely out of the building, Tug turned to Pete and said, "Inventing that story about me collecting all the other keys, that worked, in a way."

"It did," said Pete, tapping a ruler impatiently on his desk, "and it didn't."

Crossing the campus under a serene, magical May moon, with light flooding hospitably from dormitory windows, the scents of spring drifting on the air, Wexford thought, Safe again, safe again. What excitement it is to run risks, get out of tightest corners, laugh in the face of chance and danger and destruction. Mr. Pete Hallam won't dare say a word. Not since I have got the Pembroke Boys by their scrotums. And so, who is the fairest of us all? Who the most powerful member of the Class of 1946? Who supreme? Who! Wexford, that's who

11

Nobody could remember when Commencement Day had been anything but brilliant with dappled June sunshine on the campus of the Devon School, and Commencement Day 1946 was no exception. The great soaring venerable trees, full-leaved, arched gothically above the shining lawns; the sweep of courtyards and expansive commons, of playing fields and parades of Georgian buildings, radiated a quiet, settled solidity and peace.

Pete Hallam made himself breakfast in the little kitchenette in his quarters: grapefruit juice, shredded wheat, corn muffin, coffee. He was just beginning to have to watch his weight. Pete Hallam, scarecrow prisoner of war, watching his weight. The irony of that numbed his brain.

Numbed his brain. Sipping coffee at the table in the sitting room in his undershorts, Pete turned that word over in his mind: numbed, numbed.

That was what he had been ever since his wound, capture, escape, discharge, coming to Devon. He had in many ways ceased to live. He had not been able fully to believe he was alive, and probably somewhere in his subconscious he had not believed he should be alive. So many tens of millions of people had died in that terror of a war, that miasma of destruction, that he could not really *see* himself as still alive.

Or really, he could not feel it, had not been able to feel it.

Well, he was alive, he was a Master at the Devon School, a boy had just died here, violence had been loosed here, and he, Peter Hallam, was alive, on the whole well, and living in Pembroke House.

He probably had forty more years or so to live.

He was feeling healthy, this morning. The exertions of a full academic year at Devon had strengthened his leg. All that coaching, the skiing, the matchless air here, struggling with the boys and their problems and their tragedies, all of it had in the last analysis recharged something somewhere in him, something that had seemed extinguished, crushed out of existence.

There was no reason he could not go on with life. In fact he had to, had no choice. Suicide? Grotesque. Tens of millions horribly killed, and he, a blessed survivor, committing suicide?

He could take up life, he had to take up life. Where? How? With whom?

Joan Mitchell Hallam, as she persisted in calling herself, came not into his sight but into his hearing. He heard her somewhat throaty, humorous voice, saying as she had once said, "Oh Pete, come on, *grow up!*"

Joan Mitchell Hallam. Joan Hallam. They had seemed to love each other once.

Where else to start life again than at the point when it had been broken off?

It seemed incredible. So did his being alive. Joan Mitchell Hallam. Those three names strung together linked his life. The bitch had almost destroyed him. Now she thought she still loved him. He was undestroyed.

Pete found her number in his address book, and

called her up. She sounded as though she had been asleep; she also sounded very surprised and over-whelmingly happy to hear from him. "I'm still asleep," she groaned in her throaty, humorous voice. "I know I am."

⋅   ⋅   ⋅

Later, as Pete made his way across the bright cam-pus toward the Chapel, he put the pleasant conver-sation with Joan out of his mind. That, like everything else, would either flourish or die. He turned his thoughts to this school.

He reflected that the perspectives here were not merely visual. They were also historical and genera-tional, perspectives of a century and a half of boys passing through this little village, growing up at this school, making here the perilous, unshielded cross-ing from boyhood to young manhood, the trickiest transition of their lives, childhood departing from them here forever, young manhood thrust upon them while they were virtually unaware of what was hap-pening, self-ignorant half-adults, muscular youths not at all sure of what they were supposed to do with this rangy, driven person they had become. Full abruptly of rage and longing and sexual thrusts and self-questioning specters, they faced one another and the Masters and the rest of this little isolated world with all the confidence of a lion tamer at his first encounter with the beasts, flaunting panache and bravado as a thin covering for mind-freezing alarm.

And at the end of it they were graduated, stunned and delirious and muddled and exhilarated.

The Commencement ceremony was held in the Chapel. The wooden panels filling the void left by the shattered Memorial Window had been replaced by plain frosted glass, with a border strip of alternat-ing red and gray, the colors of the Devon School. There was talk of commissioning another window, but with so much else needed after years of war and austerity and shortages, the talk of replacing the window was swallowed up in other talk, to be ultimately forgotten. On the coast of Maine, Eeno Radnot was unsurprised.

The graduating class in their robes and mortarboards sat quietly and calmly at the front of the Chapel, exuding an air of healthy, optimistic involvement and anticipation. Looking at them from the west transept Pete was struck by the Eagle Scout idealism of their faces and whole demeanor, suggesting a salt-of-the-earth reliability, helpers of old ladies across streets, future chairmen of Community Chest drives, presidents of banks, probably a United States senator or two—had not Daniel Webster been a Devon boy?—founders of Boys Clubs—at least one of them would surely rescue someone from drowning—staunch and life-long leaders, dedicated to worthy causes.

As president of the class, Cotty Donaldson spoke. His theme was dedication and service to others.

Undeterred by the mysterious destruction of the Memorial Window, the Headmaster resolutely went ahead as originally planned and presented a special citation to Wexford "for organizing the unique and imaginative tribute to the young men Devon gave to the war." Going up to receive the scroll, Wexford was tall and academic-looking in his robe; Pete suddenly saw in his mind's eye Wexford receiving an honorary degree, thirty years in the future, from Oxford University, for services to humanity. Here he simply said in his well-placed voice, oratorical around the edges, with a certain smile and transparent gratitude, "Thank you."

There was a stirring final hymn and then they all filed out onto the broad steps of the Chapel, festive and exuberant in the soft and steady radiance of New Hampshire in June. The organ still thundering behind them, the graduates and their families and the faculty all responded to an inebriating sense of release. A finality had arrived, grades and standings and credits had been established forever, even the tangled threads of friendships and rivalries and hatreds and sicknesses and ignorances had reached a decisive turning point. Some surging new element of freedom, one of academia's secret powers, had been unleashed.

Nick said to Tug, "So this is what Commencement's like. Commencement. You know, I never thought of it until this minute. It means 'beginning,' doesn't it. That's a good word. Makes me feel better."

Tug said wonderingly, "I can't believe it's over."

"You mean the service or—"

"I mean everything. All of it. Everything that's happened here."

Nick looked at him, and then said slowly, "Maybe it isn't. Maybe it never really is."

Tug turned to study his brother, more adult-looking in his mortarboard, and said quizzically, "What do you mean by that?"

"I have a funny feeling we're not going to get over this, everything that happened here. I think it's built-in for life, now."

Tug contemplated him and then murmured, "You're right." They walked on in silence for a few moments, then Tug said, "Let's say good-bye to Pete Hallam. I see Cotty over there with him. Then we'll find Mum and Dad."

The Blackburn brothers, Cotty and R.T., Chet and Guy and the rest of Pembroke House gathered around the much-admired Pete, the ideal Master, athletic, wounded in the war, for high-spirited, affectionate, and quite final farewells.

• • •

Rob Willis walked out of the Chapel, and still in his graduation robe walked all the way to the Devon

River, deserted of all students and faculty, and stripping down to his shorts he dived in, and began swimming upriver, and up, and up.

• • •

The yeast of life, Pete Hallam thought as The Boys moved away, the good-bad boys, who make things happen, wreck and repair, well-meaning and uncontrolled. They run the country. That's why we have the country we have.

Wexford sailed up to him, smiling winningly.

Pete had only one thing left to say. "Congratulations on your citation."

"Thank you," replied Wexford in the same well-placed, sincere, senatorial tone. "And good-bye."

"So long," said Pete sardonically, and watched him move away, accepting congratulations as he went, placing a hand encouragingly on the shoulders of favored greeters, radiating charm and confidence as he crossed the beautiful campus toward Harvard, and then perhaps the Senate, or Sing Sing.

He's an incipient monster, thought Pete, and I can't prove it and I can't stop him. For the last dozen years we've seen in the world how monsters can come to the top and just what horrors they can achieve.

And those monsters were once adolescents.

Here there seems to be one more of them forming, and in Vladivostok or the Belgian Congo or France there are perhaps others forming, and one of these days people will have to try to cope with them, confront them, risk everything in defeating them, defeating them once again, for a time.

ABOUT THE AUTHOR

JOHN KNOWLES, a graduate of Phillips Exeter and Yale, now lives in Southampton, Long Island. He is the author of seven novels, a book on travel, and a collection of stories. Mr. Knowles is a winner of the William Faulkner Award and The Rosenthal Award of the National Institute of Arts and Letters. He lectures widely to university audiences.

If the story called A SEPARATE PEACE didn't actually "write itself", as author John Knowles states today, it was certainly a book waiting to be written and embraced, as it has been for the past 25 years. It's immense success and continued popularity prove that point. "It is a story of growth through tragedy. Young people, their deepest emotions, respond to that." Knowles appreciated the depth of his young audience's intelligence and he wrote a book that continues to satisfy generations of young readers. This book is more than a classic; it is a treasure.

☐ **A SEPARATE PEACE** 25052/$2.95

It is 1943. Gene and Phineas are roommates taking an accelerated course at the highly-respected Devon School in New Hampshire so that they can get to World War II before it's over. Both are intelligent and athletic, but while the ensuing jealousies were inevitable, the tragic consequences were not. Their story, and that of their fellow schoolmates, is one account of coming of age that is not to be missed.

☐ **PEACE BREAKS OUT** 25512/$3.50

the uneasy days of peace following World War II, senior year at the Devon School is transformed from a time of deepening friendship to one of tragic betrayal. The Baltimore Sun says of this book that it is "pleasing, disturbing, and very good indeed...not only a worthy successor to A SEPARATE PEACE, it can stand alone." This is a stunning portrayal of the darker side of the impressionable human heart.

DON'T MISS
THESE CURRENT
Bantam Bestsellers

SPECIAL
MONEY SAVING
OFFER

Now you can have an up-to-date listing of Bantam's hundreds of titles plus take advantage of our unique and exciting bonus book offer. A special offer which gives you the opportunity to purchase a Bantam book for only 50¢. Here's how!

By ordering any five books at the regular price per order, you can also choose any other single book listed (up to a $4.95 value) for just 50¢. Some restrictions do apply, but for further details why not send for Bantam's listing of titles today!

Just send us your name and address plus 50¢ to defray the postage and handling costs.